1918

WHEN THE WORLD SHOOK WITH FEAR

THE MICHELSEN STORY

J. W. BECKER

DEDICATION

This is dedicated to the Michelsen family who actually lived and lost family members during the 1918 flu pandemic. Gunda, Molly, and Mable were actually family members of mine. Gunda and Molly survived the flu epidemic, but Mabel did not. She was fourteen years old when the Flu took her.

Gunda Johanna Michelsen was my grandmother. She was the most wonderful person I've ever known. Some of what's in this book I learned from her, some is fiction, but the facts about the flu pandemic are factual. There are many similarities between the 1918 flu epidemic and the 2020 epidemic.

I started his book before the 2020 pandemic hit the world and shelfed it, but now feel it is time to release this story. I hope you enjoy it.

1

Gunda Johanna Michelsen turned eight years old in 1918. She was all knees and elbows, her unruly blond hair hung into blue eyes that twinkled with mischief. She lived with her parents, Mother Lise, Father Jaden, sisters, Molly 14, Mable 2, and her three brothers, William 4, Michael 5, and James 10 months old. They were all fair-haired children with deep blue eyes like their parents. Her mother was fond of saying that they had come from the Scandinavian Country of Norway.

"Your Grandfather, Adam was a great ship's Captain out of the port of Oksfjord. He sailed all of his life on the borders of Finland. His wife, your Grandmother, Alija was a beautiful woman. Hair as fine as gold and her eyes the color of the sky. All of you take after her. Her very name meant grace."

The Michelsen family was staunch Lutheran's and attended church regularly two blocks down from their home. They lived in Chicago, in a brick three flat on the north side of the city near Jefferson Park. The building was very old and probably should been condemned years ago. Gunda and the rest of her siblings always avoided the basement that made strange noises when you walked by. What the children didn't know was that these noises were made by the rats that lived down there.

Her father worked as a garbage collector for the city. Every morning he would go down and get out his team of draft horses and hitch them to the wagon. The horses weighed around 2000 pounds each and required a lot of care. When one of them stepped on her father's foot he limped for a month. His draft horses were named Millie and Tork. Jaden worked from sunup to sundown six days a week, and on the seventh, after church, he worked whatever other jobs he could find.

Lise took in wash and sewing to help earn money. Now that Molly was old enough she was put into service also repairing and patching. Her mother would frequently make her take out all of the stitches and redo them until she felt that they were perfect. Gunda was determined not to become part of the sewing repair team.

"Mine the little ones Gunda while Molly and I work."

"Yes, mother."

At eight years old Gunda found herself in charge of her younger siblings. She lined up her sister and brothers against the wall. She walked back and forth and looked at them.

"You have to listen to me. Mother said so, and I want you to be good and quiet children."

Ten month-old James started to crawl away from the wall. She went over, picked him up and placed him back at the wall.

"Michael, you sit down and hang on to James. The rest of you sit down too. I'm going to tell you a story."

For the next hour Gunda kept them busy by making up stories. When she got tired and couldn't think of anything else to tell them she said it was time for them to take a nap.

The apartment was small with only three bedrooms, a combination kitchen and living room. There was also a small room off of the living room that Gunda called 'the fireplace home.' Sometimes she would go there just to be alone, but she never had the courage to light a fire.

Her mother and father had the small bedroom in the front of the house. The three girls shared one bed in an even tinier room and the boys had their bed in the other room. The only thing that fit into these rooms were the beds. The one dresser outside the room was shared by all six children. They were assigned one drawer each except James and William who shared a drawer. The children's bedrooms butted up against each other. Sometimes at night they would knock on the wall and giggle until mother came and yelled at them to go to sleep.

The three boys climbed into the bed together. Mable said she didn't want to sleep alone so Gunda placed her in with the boys. She waited until they were asleep before going to see what her mother wanted. She wanted her to go to the neighborhood store.

Her mother gave her a list of things that she wanted from the store. It read, bread, eggs, milk, and porridge. "Here's $.51 that should be enough money. Come right home when you're done."

"I'll be back before they get up from their nap Mother."

"Wait. Come back here Gunda. There's something else I need that you can get for me. Lise went over to the buffet that sat next to the kitchen and rummaged through it. She carefully pulled out a small pouch and folded something into her palm. She bent down and whispered to Gunda, "Give this to Mr. Poll; he'll know what it's for."

Gunda opened her hand and saw the $.50 her mother had placed in it. "Mother?"

"Go on now. Mother needs her medicine."

2

Gunda walked down the paper strewn street. She briefly wondered where all the papers came from and why someone didn't clean them up. Sometimes she would collect the papers and try to read them. She didn't understand a lot of what the Chicago Sun-Times said, but once in a while she found the funny pages and shared them with her brothers and sisters. She didn't have time to look at the papers right now and walked quickly over to Anthony Street, followed that to Crompton and took a left to Wells Street.

The Shadowland Grocery sat at the bottom portion of a red brick building on the corner of the block. The store was owned by John Poll. It was a convenient store in the neighborhood that Gunda new well. Her mother often sent here for groceries and her medicine.

She skipped through the door and yelled, "Hi, Mr. Poll."

Mr. Poll was a 50-year-old black man who had run the store for the last 25 years. Gunda called him the gentle giant because he stood six-foot four and reminded her of a teddy bear. She liked this man who always had a smile for her and laughed at the dumb jokes of an 8 year old.

"How are you this fine day, Miss Gunda?"

"I'm well. Thank you, sir." She laughed. "Mother sent me for milk, eggs, bread and porridge."

"Well now, Honey, I think we can handle that order. Let's go find you the freshest of that bread."

After John gathered her groceries and place them in a bag he held out a licorice whip.

"I don't have money for that."

"Don't need money. It's a gift. You're my friend and I want to give it to you."

Gunda grinned. "Thank you."

"You go on straight home now. I heard there are problems in the street. Bad man's walking."

"What does that mean? Bad man walking?"

"One that hurts little ones. Best be alert. Don't want anyone to get my Gunda doll."

Gunda smiled, he was the only one that ever called her that, his little Gunda doll. It always made her feel good inside.

"That little Nancy child....."

"Nancy Wilson?" Gunda interrupted.

"That's the child. She's in the hospital. Was hurt bad by that man walking. At least that's what I heard on the streets."

"Nancy is in my class at school."

"You just be careful child."

"Yes Sir, I surely will."

"How's the family doing? Your daddy still working?"

"Father is always working. We hardly see him at all. Oh," Gunda dug into her pocket and pulled out the $.50 her mother had given her. "Mother needs....... you know........ from in the back."

John shook his head and clucked, "Poor lady. Poor lady. You wait here."

Gunda waited until John came out from the back room. He had a paper bag in his hand with a bottle neatly tucked in it. He handed it to her. "Here you go."

When Gunda walked into the house her mother grabbed the bottle and went to her bedroom leaving the grocery's to her and the rest of the mending to Molly. She would down the whiskey before the sun was set. Five minutes later she would be asleep leaving Molly with Gunda's help to feed the children.

When her father came home Molly placed a plate of scrambled eggs and piece of bread in front of him. He never said a word, ate the eggs and then got up and went straight to bed. Molly washed the dishes while Gunda got the little ones ready for bed.

Everyone was asleep but Gunda and Molly. They sat at the small table in the kitchen. Gunda took out the licorice whip that John had given her and split it with Molly. She told her about Nancy.

"They told us at school about the man who was grabbing kids and making them disappear." Molly said as she took a bite out of the licorice whip.

"Nancy Wilson didn't disappear."

"She was lucky. So far there are three missing. They're all in my class, Carol Saints, Melissa Gold, and Mary States. It's like they just disappeared. It's been about three months or more."

"You think someone stole them?"

"I don't know. Let's go get some sleep. Tomorrow is a school day for you."

"Aren't you going?"

Molly eyes moved to her mother's bedroom door, "Mother needs me to do some sewing. She doesn't think she can do it all alone and it has to be done by Tuesday."

~~~
~~~

The walk to school seemed odd to Gunda. Molly had always walked with her. Now it was just her and Michael. She hung tightly onto his hand. He was starting kindergarten today and she had to make sure that he got there. The kindergarten room was on the first floor. When they got in front of the door she bent down and straightened Michael's shirt collar.

"I'll be back to get you after school. You wait right here for me."

"Can you come in with me?"

"All right, but then I have to go to my class."

Normally her mother would be the one to take Michael to his first day of school, but she was 'sick' again. When they left she was still in bed.

Gunda introduced herself to Miss Goman, the kindergarten teacher. "It's Michael's first day and he was a little jittery."

"Do you mean that he's nervous?"

"Yes ma'am. That too."

Lillian Goman looked at this tattered little girl in a dress that was too big for her. Her blonde hair hung haphazardly down her back and the left shoe on her foot had no shoelace. She would bet that her shoes were laced with newspaper where they were worn out. The boy, Michael wasn't in much better shape. His pant legs had ripped across the knee and were folded at the ankles. The faded shirt he wore was too big. She told Michael to sit down and took Gunda out into the hall.

"Your mother is supposed to bring Michael the first day. Where is she?"

"She couldn't come. She's been sick."

"When she gets better would you tell her that I'd like to talk with her?"

"Yes ma'am, I surely well."

Gunda watched Miss Goman walk back into the kindergarten room before she left. She would have to avoid her and meet Michael on the playground. She knew that her mother would never come to school.

3

It was Saturday. Gunda had just put James down for a nap and gathered her other two brothers to go with her on what she deemed an adventure. She asked Molly if she wanted to come along but she said that all she wanted to be was left alone. She was in a hurry to finish the sewing so that she could go out later and it was none of Gunda's business where she was going. Their father had gone off to a second job to help Mr. Peter Weston at the junkyard. Her mother was once again in bed with her sickness and wouldn't get up.

There was a knock at the door. Molly stopped sewing and went to answer it while Gunda put breakfast on the table. Breakfast today was a piece of toast and a spoonful of porridge for each child.

"Good morning, Mrs. Stanley." Molly said smiling broadly at the landlady.

Mrs. Stanley was a woman of few words. "Where's your mother or father?"

"Father's working. My mother isn't here right now." She lied.

Gunda couldn't believe that Molly had just told a big, fat lie to Mrs. Stanley. She cautioned her brothers not to say anything. They all knew that Lise was in bed with her sickness. She was dead drunk at 9 o'clock in the morning.

While Molly talked to Mrs. Stanley, Gunda told the others to hurry and eat because she had a surprise for them when they were done. She carefully watched Molly while she was talking to the landlady. She could tell by the positioning of her body whatever she was being told was not good. Even at eight years old she knew that there was trouble coming their way.

Molly quickly and quietly closed the door behind the landlady. Gunda went over to her and asked, "What did she want?"

Molly sat down at the table and lowered her head into her hands. "The rent. She said father didn't pay the rent."

Gunda hesitated before she asked "how much is it?"

"She wants ten dollars and she wants it by tomorrow."

"Maybe he just forgot. He'll pay her when he gets home."

Gunda placed Molly's cup of porridge in front of her with the half piece of bread. "I hate porridge."

Gunda slid back into her chair and picked up her piece of bread. William looked longingly at it. She handed it to him.

"Molly how much does a job of work pay?"

"It depends on the type of work. I think father gets about $.15 an hour, but I'm not sure. I read in one of those papers you brought home that Mr. President Woodrow Wilson was trying to get something called the minimum wage so people can get more money for work."

"What's minimum wage?"

"I'm not sure."

Michael sat down to join them. "Why can't father stay home with us? We hardly see him anymore?"

"Because he has to work so we can live here."

"If we didn't live here where would we live?"

"I don't know."

Molly flicked her finger against Michael head. "Don't ask so many questions and eat your bread."

Michael put his head down and started to cry. Gunda put her arm around her little brother and said, "Don't worry about it. We're not going anywhere. Let's go help Willie get dressed and we'll go on an adventure.

"What's an adventure?"

"It's kind of like when you do something different. Something new. Something we've never done before." Gunda leaned down close to Michael and whispered in his ear. "Something dangerous."

Michael's eyes widened. "Really?"

"Really. Run and get dressed."

Molly had been listening to every word that Gunda said. "Don't get far." She yelled as she went back to finish her sewing."

"We won't. We'll probably go to the park over by the big hill."

At the last minute Willie decided that he didn't want to go and crawled in bed with their mother. He said that he wasn't feeling good. When he shook Lise she groaned and turned over but never woke up.

"Just go." Molly said. "I'll watch William, Mable and James. You better be home before dark."

"Are you going out with Henry again?"

"I might."

"Father wouldn't like it if he knew."

"Well, if you keep your big mouth shut he won't know, will he?"

"Okay. I'm going to check on Willie before I go."

Gunda went over to her mother's bed and looked down at her. She knew that she had been drinking again and probably wouldn't wake up for a while. She gently touched Willie's cheek.

She was the only one who called him Willie. "Are you okay Willie?"

"I'm tired."

"Go to sleep then. I'll be home later and Molly will be staying with you today."

"Okay." The little boy yawned and turned over.

Gunda went over to the table next to her mother and father's bed. She carefully opened the drawer and picked up an old red sock that lay inside. She knew that her father gave her mother $1.50 every week to run the house. Since he rarely ate at home she wondered if he knew that their meals were mostly bread and porridge. The rest of the money went to mothers 'medicine.'

She emptied the coins into the palm of her hand. There was $2.15. She had never had that much money in her hands before. The silver felt cool against her skin. She hesitated before she took out $1.10. Now, she thought, I'm a thief. It didn't bother her too much because she reasoned that if they did get kicked out of the apartment money would be very important.

She learned at a very young age how important money actually was. There was a time when they had lived on the streets and she never wanted to be put in that situation again, or go back to that life. She was 4 years old at the time and it was still clear in her mind. The hunger. The fear at night. The crying people and babies.

Back then it was only her, Mother, Father, Molly, and Michael. Her mother was pregnant at the time with William. They wound up living in a camp near the beach across from Lake Michigan. Groups of homeless people came together on an open three-acre plot of land. They had lived there for five months in a makeshift tent, eating whatever her mother or father could scrounge up. Some days they had nothing to eat.

One day father came back to the tent city and said that he had found a place for them to live. He took them to the apartment that they now shared. Father would never tell where he got the money for the apartment, but she heard her mother and father fighting about it. After that night it was never discussed again.

Gunda learned from an early age that not having money was probably the worst thing in the world that could happen to someone. She decided then that she would always have money. At every opportunity she would take a few dimes or a nickel from her mother's purse and hide it. After a while she decided that her mother could hardly keep track of her own kids so she would not miss a few pennies here and there. Taking this much may be a mistake. She shrugged and shoved the money into her pocket.

Gunda lied to Molly because she knew if she told where they were really going she would try to stop her. Gunda took Michael to Lake Michigan and showed him where they used live years ago. She wasn't surprised that the camp was still there. As her father had always told her ..... "Times were hard and people did what they had to."

She took Michael's hand and walked with him through the homeless camp trying to remember when her little brother, William was born. They lived there sharing one tent. When her mother's time came there was no doctor, only a woman from another tent who came to help her. The first thing she did was place all of them outside. Molly, Gunda, and one-year-old Michael were told to stay out. They held hands as they walked around the camp several times before going back to sit outside of their own tent.

Gunda will never forget the low moaning and screams that came from the tent. No one else seemed to notice as they were going about their own day. When she questioned Molly about what was happening she told her to shut up. It seemed to take all night before her brother was born, but it didn't end there. The baby wasn't right. He was born with a bluish color. Jaden was convinced by Mrs. Madison, the midwife, to take William to the hospital.

Only one resident in tent city had a car. Mr. Groote insisted he couldn't drive him unless he could come up with a dollar for gas. Jaden didn't have a dollar.

Mrs. Madison immediately went into action and collected nickels and pennies from several families. She managed to come up with $.87. She shoved it at Mr. Groote.

"Take this money and get that poor baby to the hospital. You want that poor babe to die?"

Mr. Groote was 72 years old and had been living in the city for the last five years. Every day had become a struggle and the last thing he cared about was some baby, but he had to live with these people so he thought he'd better help.

"Okay. I guess $.87 will work okay."

The old man pocketed the money and grunted. "Come on. Hurry it up. The lady that comes with the bread will be here soon and I don't want to miss her."

Jaden had wrapped William in his coat. Lise was too weak to accompany them to the hospital.

"Keep him warm." Mrs. Madison advised." And don't worry about your Missus; I'll stay with her until you return."

Mr. Groote didn't drive Jaden all the way to the hospital. He ran out of gas several blocks away. He turned to Jaden who was sitting in the backseat with William. "That's it. Can't get no further. Got no more gas."

"Go get some."

"No place around here. Got to walk far for gas. I'm heading back. Hospital is two blocks that way." He said pointing to the south.

Jaden had no choice so he got out of the car and tucked William close to his chest before he started to walk. The weather had turned colder and he ducked his head close in an attempt to keep the baby warm. William didn't cry and that worried him. All of his babies had cried when they were born.

Jaden walked into the hospital's emergency room department. The entire waiting room was full with people in various stages of illness or injury. He had never been in a hospital before and wasn't sure how to proceed. All of his children had been birthed at home by midwives. He saw a woman dressed all in white standing behind a desk.

He walked over there and said, "excuse me, ma'am. My baby is sick."

The nurse, whose name tag said Ellen Tucker came around the counter and peered into the jacket that William was wrapped in. When she saw the babies blue coloring she took him from Jaden. "Stay here. The doctor will come to talk to you."

She disappeared down the corridor into a back room. Jaden didn't know what else to do so he joined the other people that were sitting in the waiting room.

Twenty minutes later Jaden was taken to a room where Dr. Gills explained to him that William was suffering from 'blue baby syndrome.'

"Your baby will need to stay in the hospital. He has reduced hemoglobin in his blood."

"Don't think I understand."

"He doesn't have enough oxygen in his blood and that's what is causing his blue color. It's very treatable, but he must stay. My real concern is his rapid heartbeat. I want to try to reverse that."

"Boy can't stay Doc. Got no money for it."

"This is a county hospital. We will take care of your son and there will be no cost to you."

William stayed for a week in the hospital. Jaden walked from tent city every day to the hospital. Finally, he was allowed to come home, but the doctor cautioned him that he had to return to the clinic with him every week. Jaden agreed but knew that it would never happen.

William was always a fussy baby and had trouble eating. Gunda worked the best with him and sometimes she spent an hour just trying to get him to eat some food. He had trouble understanding things and sometimes had to be told several times before he could accomplish in the simplest of tasks. He tired easily and always seemed to be sickly. All of these memories flooded into her mind. It was time for them to leave. This place only brought her sadness.

Gunda and Michael walked the two blocks down to Lake Michigan. When they got there they walked across the sand and she pointed to the lake. "Take off your shoes and walk along the water."

"I've never seen so much water. How far does it go? I can't see to the other side?"

"I'm not sure, but you would have to ride for a long, long, long time before you ever got to the other side. Years maybe."

Today it seemed like summer was in the air. The sun was shining and the heat beat down on them. Bright blue skies washed down to the waves and moved against the sand leaving behind water droplets that looked like small pieces of glass running along the shoreline. She walked into the water with Michael and pointed. Tiny fish darted back and forth rushing nowhere. Michael giggled wildly and pointed at them.

"Let's see if we can catch some of them."

For the next hour they jumped in the water and chased the little silver fish but never caught one. It was a fine game they played until the weather turned. The bright skies became dark with clouds that slowly crept across it. The wind started to blow pushing at the water and sand turning it a dark color with the coolness of the evening. Gunda felt the summer heat slide away and goose bumps ran across her arms. It had been a good day for them and probably the last one they would have before the coldness of winter came.

"I think it's time we go." Gunda said as she helped Michael with his shoes.

They started for home. They had gone part of the way before they managed to hitch a ride. It would be dark when they arrived home.

Molly couldn't wait any longer; she had to talk to Henry immediately. She had gone into the bedroom and shook Lise, but she was too drunk to respond. She went back into the kitchen area. "William, listen very carefully to me, you stay with mother. Gunda will be home soon. Don't touch anything or when I come back I'll spank you. Mable and James are sleeping together in the crib. Don't wake them."

William looked at her wide-eyed. Molly knew he didn't understand a word she said to him. She grabbed her hat and ran out the door. He went over and looked into the crib and then lay down on the floor next to it. He put his thumb in his mouth and closed his eyes.

Jaden had brought the crib home from the junkyard. He had done his best to fix the broken slats. He took the wood from the lumber yard and stole the saw, hammer and nails. He was used to stealing what he needed. It had become a habit. When he was done he looked at the crib, it wasn't very pretty, but it worked.

When Gunda got home she couldn't believe that Molly had left, just left the children alone. As mad as Molly was so was she. She was also angry with her mother. She didn't understand how she could lay in bed like that and sleep all the time.

After she made the porridge for their dinner, (Gunda vowed that when she got old she would never eat the hated porridge again) she went into her mother's bedroom. She looked at Lise; she was sprawled out on the bed with a brown paper bag next to her. She picked up the bag and smelled the foul odor of alcohol. She dropped the bag next to the bed and shook her mother.

"What?" Lise slurred. "What?"

"Mother you need to get up. It's late. Where's father?"

"How the hell do I know?" She sniffed loudly, "work. Go way."

She plopped back down on the bed and started to snore. Gunda threw her hands up in the air. She knew that it was no use because she wouldn't be able to get her up. She would probably sleep until tomorrow.

4

Molly met with Henry at the corner of Jefferson and State. Henry was 17 years old and thought he could do no wrong. He had on a pair of dirty jeans, white shirt and a leather jacket. His longer brown hair hung into his eyes.

"Where'd you get the jacket?" Molly asked.

"Guy gave it to me."

The guy who gave Henry the jacket was Dietrich Combs. He gave it to Henry because he had threatened him with a switchblade. After Henry got the jacket from him he pushed him down, knelt on his chest and cut his ear as a reminder not to talk.

Molly was extremely nervous about what she had to tell Henry. She attempted to smile and said, "It's a nice jacket."

"Yeah. Okay. Spill. What's so important we had to meet tonight?"

Henry always seemed to have money so she asked him if they could go somewhere to sit down and talk. "Sure, let's go to Jane's Place."

Jane's place was a small hole in the wall restaurant. It had two tables and four chairs at a counter. There were paper signs taped to the wall with prices. They went in and sat down on one of the tables and Henry yelled, "Hey Janie, two cokes over here."

Jane was very heavy set and around 70 years old. She wore an old blue checked dress and a yellow scarf around her neck. She waddled over and placed the two glasses down in front of Henry.

"That's $.14."

He reached into his pocket and flipped out two dimes. "Keep it." Henry turned back to Molly, "okay, Honey Bee, what's up?"

"Please don't call me that."

Henry leaned way back in the chair and eyed her suspiciously. "Okay, baby. What's up?"

Molly couldn't hold it in one minute longer. She looked Henry straight in the eye and said, "I'm pregnant."

Henry didn't say a word. He just smiled. "Why tell me?"

"Because it's your baby." She whispered.

"No way. Don't try to pin this on me."

"Henry!"

"Don't Henry me. The kids not mine. Go find someone else to accuse."

"Henry, it is your baby. I've been with no one else." Henry grabbed Molly by the shirt front. He slid into the booth next to her and pulled her close squeezing tightly. "Listen carefully; there is no way I'm going to get saddled with you and your kid. If you don't want it................ get rid of it." He snarled.

Molly couldn't believe what she was hearing. All she could do was sputter, "what?"

"You heard me. I'm no one's daddy."

"Henry, I don't know what to do here. Please, you have to help me."

"Okay, I'll help you."

Henry grabbed her by the arm and pulled her out of the restaurant door and over to the alley next door to it. He pinned her against the wall and leaned in real close and snarled at her again. "No kid. Not for me. I don't want you to come around here anymore. Don't be bother me about a kid that isn't mine. You are nothing to me. I got a woman and it's not you." He slammed her hard against the wall. "Don't come back or you're dead." He flashed his switchblade at her, turned and walked away.

Molly stood in the alley against the wall for the next 10 minutes. She was stunned and so numb that she couldn't even move. All kinds of thoughts were running through her head. She was 14, pregnant, and had no money. Even if she would want to get an abortion she couldn't pay for it and she had no idea how to go about it.

She lived with her parents and five siblings in a three room apartment. There was always a struggle. There was never enough money to pay the rent or to buy food. Her father was never home because all he did was work. Her mother was a drunk. She spent most of her waking hours sewing to make pennies. How could she have been so stupid? How could she bring another mouth to be fed into the house? How could she tell her father?

~~~

It was way past dark when Molly came home. Gunda was waiting for her. She grabbed her when she walked through the door. She had the rest of the kids stashed in the boy's bedroom. She hurried Molly across the living room, past the kitchen and into their empty bedroom. From the other side of the hall they could hear Jaden and Lise screaming at each other. Molly looked down the hallway and then ducked back into the bedroom, "what happened?"

"When father came home there was nothing to eat. Nothing but porridge. He wanted to know why and I told him that mother didn't have any money left, and then Willey started. He wet himself and then threw himself on the ground screaming. You know how he can be. I've never seen father so angry. He started yelling at mother about no food in the house. He found her bottle. She was hiding it
~~~

in the bed with her. They have been hollering at each other ever since."

"We better just stay here. There's nothing we can do."

"Father said he got her a job at the shoe factory on something called an assembly line. She got real mad and said she wasn't going to go there and stand on her feet all day for a few lousy dollars. Molly, he told her if she didn't take the job she could just get out not come back."

"He's just mad. He doesn't really mean it."

Molly and Gunda went to bed that night hearing the echoes of angry voices. Her mother finally agreed that she would work in the factory and that seem to lower the level of their anger.

Molly couldn't sleep, she was confused and frightened. If father could become so angry about a job, what would he do if she told him that she was pregnant? If she told him she was pregnant would he tell her to leave? Where would she go? Henry wouldn't help her. She had no money. She remembered when she was homeless and lived in a tent. How could she do that with a baby?

She thought about telling her mother but knew that her only interest was in a bottle. She couldn't turn to her church because in their eyes she was a sinner. A tainted woman for being with child and not married. There was nowhere to turn. Nowhere to go. Molly looked down at her stomach. It was still flat so she had a little time before she had to make a decision. She turned into her pillow and cried.

~~~

Father was gone all weekend. He told the children that he had picked up an extra job. Molly was put in charge because mother would be working at the factory. Before he left he brought home some groceries. Bread, milk, eggs, and surprise, a jar of jelly for the
~~~

bread. Gunda couldn't remember the last time they had jelly with their bread.

When father came home with the groceries, Gunda and Molly were sitting at the table with several pairs of shoes lined up in front of them. They were tearing pieces of newspaper that Gunda had collected throughout the week. They were going to use them to line the bottoms of their shoes. Gunda had a hole in her left shoe that she was working on. It was getting colder and soon the snow would fall. She hated when her feet got wet.

They were also going through all the old coats they had. Molly's coat was too small for her so she gave it to Gunda. She had two sweaters and that would have to do. If it got really cold she would have to stay home. They would go through the small assortment of things they had and see if the other kids would be able to use any of them. Hopefully, coats could be passed down to the next child in line.

Everyone cooperated with this project except little James. He was sleepy and cranky. Molly warmed the last of the milk and put a weak portion of porridge in it before putting him to bed.

Jaden strolled into the kitchen and looked at the small pile of clothes that were next to them and the shoes on the table.

"What's all this?"

"Were fixing holes in our shoes and seeing who can fit into our winter coats."

Jaden picked up Gunda's shoe and turned it over. He didn't say a word, just nodded and walked out the door. He was going to another job.

~ ~ ~

Gunda heard William crying in the next room. She went over to the boy's room and helped him out of bed. They walked into the living room and she sat down with William on the floor. She put her arm around him and said, "Don't cry Little Willie."

"Willie wet."

Gunda knew exactly what Willie had said. He had peed on himself again. "Okay. You wait here. I'll be right back." She searched through James's stack of clothes and found a diaper. She pulled it out and went back to Willie. She placed a sweater under his head and pulled off his wet pants.

"You'll have to wear this because all of your stuff is dirty right now."

Once he was dry Willie didn't care what he was wearing. He rolled over and put his thumb into his mouth and closed his eyes. Gunda covered him with a blanket and let him sleep where he was.

Gunda looked up when she heard the front door open. She was surprised to see her father had come home. It was still early in the morning. He had a big box in his hands that he placed next to the kitchen table.

"What are you doing up?"

"Willie wet his pants."

"Come and sit with me."

Gunda sat down at the table across from her father. "I'm really worried about Willie. He's not as good as he was before."

"What does that mean?"

"Well, he wets his pants all the time now, and he has trouble swallowing his food sometimes. He doesn't talk so much. He didn't do that stuff before."

Jaden looked at his daughter and he thought how this is a conversation he should be having with Willie's mother, not her. "How long has this been going on?"

"I'm not sure father."

"What does your mother say about this?"

"She doesn't say anything. Most of the time she just stays in the bed."

Jaden took Gunda's hand in his. "You're so good with Willie. I count on you to take care of him. If things get worse with Willie let me know. I brought some winter things for everyone. They're in the box."

Jaden was tired, he got up, patted her on the head and then went to bed. Gunda was confused. She always took care of Willie, but she thought he was in trouble now and needed her father's help. She guessed that she would just have to keep taking care Willie and hope that things didn't get worse.

Gunda thought about Michael who was only a year older and he did a lot more things then Willie. He could read a little, tie his own shoes, feed himself, and even dress himself if he had to. Willie couldn't do any of that by himself. If she didn't coax him to eat he probably wouldn't do that either.

Gunda went over to the box and opened it up. Inside she found shoes and coats. They were all new. Most of them still had store tags on them. She knew that father had no money for all of these clothes and wondered how he got these things. She picked up each of the coats and hugged them to her. They would be so nice and warm for the winter. She also looked at the shoes; everything was in various sizes so that it would fit each of them.

The roar of thunder rocked the windows and rain started to pelt the building. She quickly decided that she didn't care where the shoes and coats came from because in a few weeks it would be much colder. These coats would keep them warm. It was better not to ask questions.

5

Lise dragged herself out of bed and grunted. She shook her head to try to clear it. Jaden was going to walk her to the new factory job and introduce it to her boss, Mr. Ronald Byrd.

Before they left, Jaden gave Molly money to get food for the children. He told Molly that she would be in charge and she would have to watch the children today until they could make other arrangements. There would be no school for her. After their parents left Molly handed the money to Gunda.

"You go down the Shadowland Grocery and I'll stay here with the kids."

"What about school?"

"Forget it."

The weather had turned cold during the night with rain. Gunda picked out a red coat that Jaden had brought home and put it on. While she hurried over to the grocery store she thought about her home. For some reason she had a bad feeling about everything that was going on. Jaden and Lise were always fighting now. The fights were about money, Lise's drinking and Willie. Jaded wanted to take him back to the hospital not only because he was regressing, but he seemed to be sick all the time. He didn't want to play and just stayed in bed most of the time. Gunda had tried to coax him to eat, but he refused. Finally she took one of James's bottles and made a very weak porridge mix like she did for the baby. She offered it to Willie, he managed to take a small portion of it at a time. She still worried because it took her all day to get him just to finish that one bottle and she knew that that wasn't enough.

Before she left Gunda took a dollar from her money stash. She would ask John Poll if there was some medicine that she could get for Willie. She got the old wagon from under the stairs to carry the groceries home because she would probably not be able to carry them all by herself.

When she got to the store she was surprised that John wasn't there. She called out to him, "Mr. Poll. It's Gunda. Are you here?"

John came from the back room and smiled at the little girl. She thought he looked awful. He moved so slowly and his eyes were bloodshot.

"Are you sick?"

"Not too bad. Just feel a little poorly today. Caught me a cold. Have you come for some more groceries?"

"Yes Sir."

Gunda decided she wouldn't bother Mr. Poll with Willies problems when he was feeling so bad. "I'll get everything I need. You just sit down." She gathered the eggs, milk, bread, and porridge fixings that she needed. She decided to buy some soup because it would be easy for Willie to eat and added it to her wagon.

"That's 62 cents."

Gunda counted the change twice. She was five cents short so she pulled out the extra from her money. Before she left John asked, "How's things at your house?"

"Everything's pretty good except Willies not eating very well, that's why I got the soup."

"Hold on now, child, maybe I got something that can help."

John came back with a small bottle of corn syrup. "Put a few drops in his porridge. Mix it in real good and it'll make it sweet. He will be more likely to eat it."

"How much is it?"

"Don't you worry about it. You just take it and go on now."

"Are you sure?"

"Absolutely sure."

"Thank you, Mr. Poll. I'll see you in a few days."

Gunda didn't know that it would be the last time she would see her friend. John Poll died that night. He had gotten ill in the morning and died within an eight hour period.

When Gunda got home she struggled to carry all the groceries to the third floor apartment. She didn't know that once she stepped through the door her life would change dramatically. It was September 1918 and John Pall's illness was about to grip the entire world. Gunda had been exposed the minute she entered the grocery store.

6

The big question in September of 1918 was when and how the 1918 Global Flu Pandemic started and where did it come from. The when and where are not positively known and probably will never be. The reality was that by the time it would all be over more than 50 million people throughout the world would succumb to the disease. Some estimates actually rose to more than that. Officials at the time claimed as many as 100 million had died. It was at that time and to this day considered the world's worst plague to across the world.

THE WORLD'S WORST PLAGED

The flu epidemic of 1918 was also known as the Spanish flu. Some estimated that as many as 500 million (28%) of the world's population came down with this illness. The disease crossed the world and merged into a deadly killer. After it started it marched through the year of 1918 and into 1919 killing people worldwide.

It was estimated that it killed more people than World War 1 (WW1). The pandemic was known as one of the worst disasters that had ever befallen man.

Someone who got the flu could also have secondary problems of pneumonia. This lead to a secondary bacterial infection as the disease progressed. It was considered a fast death because people who were ill in the morning would die by nightfall. One of the strangest things about the disease was that people seemed to be disappearing and were never heard from again, something that was never explained.

As World War I came to an end soldiers in US camps were coming down with the virus. Soon it was spread throughout the European campaign. One of the first reports of the disease came from a military installation, Fort Riley.

Sargent Major Greystone came home from Europe, the Western front, with the beginnings of flu. Before he returned to the United States he infected Sgt. Phil Carla who infected Corporal Mark Experts. Each of these men would spread the disease to everyone they came in contact with. It had only taken days for hundreds of soldiers to become sick with the flu. Soon other military camps reported the disease as it spread rapidly throughout them. After that, the entire general population of the world had been exposed.

The first to succumb to the disease were the elderly and the very young, but it was noted that younger people who contacted the disease also died quicker. No one could give an explanation for this, but the group between the ages of 20 and 40 seem to be most vulnerable.

The disease attacked quickly and deadly. The disease attacked the lungs building up fluid that seeped into them. Accumulation of fluid into the lungs suffocated the victims.

~~~

It was thought that this flu came to Chicago when sailors from the Great Lakes Naval Training Station suddenly became ill. It was the start of what would be a city wide epidemic. Great Lakes attempted to isolate the disease by using quarantine controls, restricting the sailors and closing off the base. Their efforts did little to stop the spread of the disease.

By this time the flu had spread throughout Chicagoland. There was a remarkable amount of deaths reported just due to respiratory problems. The health commissioner, Mr. Robertson
~~~

ordered immediate isolation for the cases that came into the Cook County Hospital. As the disease quickly spread the city was coming to a fast halt.

People were told to go home and stay there and not to be in public anymore the necessary. Oddly enough the schools were allowed to remain open because attendance had not been interrupted and it was nearly normal. That soon came to an end. People were arrested for coughing in public and not covering their mouths. They would be brought before a judge and lectured on the dangers of the flu before being released.

Soon all public places were shutting down. Most schools that had been open were closing. Theaters, churches, restaurants, and public buildings closed their doors.

Public funerals were prohibited which led to caskets being stored in family homes. Cases of the flu were reported at more than 1200 a day.

Chicago was ordered by the health commissioner to close their boarders. The lost revenue was estimated to go up into the millions of dollars.

The flu wasn't the only disease being dealt with. As the flu raged on people became suicidal leaving behind families to defend for themselves. After suffering mental breakdowns, husbands in their desperation killed their wives and children.

High fevers brought with it its own type of insanity. Herbert Cummings ravished with fever and out of his senses shot himself with a revolver. Fathers were killing their children and wife's killed their husbands.

The death toll rose as whole families died within days of getting the disease. It was not uncommon to find caskets lined up inside family rooms of homes. This pandemic would kill more people than the Black Death.

Those who didn't die out right of the flu were dying of the secondary infection, pneumonia. It was even thought that many deaths were caused because of aspirin poisoning. People were taking large amounts of it as part of their treatment and unknown to them they were killing themselves with it.

Healthcare workers couldn't keep up with the sick. Gravediggers also couldn't keep up with the dead. Mass graves were dug and as a result many bodies were buried without coffins or gravestones. People were gripped with fear. Chicago was becoming deserted as people hid in fear.

~ ~ ~

When Gunda got home she told Molly about John Poll. "He said he was sick and was closing the store for a while so I asked him if we could double up on the groceries. It was a good thing I took the wagon. We owe him some more money. I told him father would pay him next week."

"Why did you do that?"

"Because the next store is over a mile away."

"Willie's sick. I can't get him to eat anything. Maybe you should try."

Gunda went into the boy's bedroom. Willie had completely covered his head with a blanket. Two-year-old Mable was sleeping next to him. Gunda pulled back the cover and smiled at Willie.

"Hi Willie. I brought you a bottle."

"No."

"You have to eat something."

"Hurts."

"What hurts?"

Gunda was used to Willie's one-word answers. He didn't talk much at all anymore. Willie pointed to his head and she put her hand on it. She was surprised at how hot he felt. She went to get Molly.

Molly felt Willie's head. "He is hot. I think he has a fever."

"When will father be home?"

"How would I know? I think Mother should be here soon."

Gunda would rather have her father because at least he cared what happened to them. All her mother cared about was where her next bottle would come from.

Molly handed Gunda the baby bottle. "Try again. Get him to eat something."

Gunda wondered why Molly was in such a bad mood, but having a little kid sick and tending to the needs of two others would probably make her cranky too. "I'll try.

Lise came in an hour later and was in a very foul mood. She had spent all day on that hot assembly-line in which she considered the most boring job in the entire world. She needed a drink. When Gunda looked at her mother she realized that she had forgotten her whiskey bottle.

Lise zeroed in on Gunda. "Where is it?"

The little girl backed away from her and said in a quiet voice. "I forgot it. Mr. Poll, he was sick and wanted to go back to bed and......... And I forgot it."

Lise reached out and slapped her hard across the face. Gunda actually went down to her knees and when she looked up at her mother there were tears in her eyes.

Molly stepped in front of Gunda. "Mother! Stop!"

Lise held up her fist. "You want some of this. I need my medicine and she didn't get it."

Jaden opened the door and quickly stepped in when he saw Lise with her hand raised toward the children.

"LISE! What's going on here?"

"The kid didn't get my medicine that's what's going on here."

Jaden took several steps over to Lise and grabbed her arm. "Booze! You hit the kid because she didn't get you a bottle. Are you crazy? Don't you ever touch the children again!" As he talked his voice kept raising until he was finally screaming at her. "Never."

Jaden pushed Lise out of the way and helped Gunda up from the floor. He hugged her quickly and stomped off after Lise. She couldn't have been more surprised if he had hit her too. Jaden was not much for affection.

Molly took Mable from the boy's bedroom and put her into the crib with James. She reached over and felt Willie's head again, he felt hotter. "Gunda, go get Father."

Gunda lightly knocked at the door of her parents' bedroom. She could hear them arguing and knocked louder.

Her mother's screaming voice greeted her. "What?"

"Willie's sick. I think father needs to come and see him. His head is really hot."

Jaden came out of the bedroom and went down the hall to Willie's room. He leaned down to the bed and called to him. "Willie."

When the boy didn't answer he sat down next to him. He was alarmed when he felt the warmth in him. His entire body seemed to be burning with fever.

"Molly, get some cool water and rags. Gunda you go see if there's any aspirin left in the kitchen drawer."

When Molly came back with the water and rags she handed them to Jaden. He pulled down the covers and placed a cold rag across Willie's chest. Gunda handed him the aspirin, but Willie refused to take it.

"I have an idea."

Gunda went to the kitchen, took the aspirin and crushed it on the table. She poured milk into what was now considered Willie's baby bottle and put the crushed aspirin into the bottle. She knew that this was the only way she could get Willie to eat. She shook it vigorously. At the last minute she remembered the sweet syrup John had given her and added a teaspoon to the mixture. She shook the bottle again.

Gunda went back to the bedroom and crawled up next to Willie. "Here Willie," she cooed. "Try this. It's really good." After about an hour she had managed to get him to drink half of the bottle.

7

The newspapers had been filled with stories about the killer that stuck Chicago. Almost every day there was another theory about what and why it was happening. People were continuing to disappear. They were of all ages and all races so it was hard for the police to try to connect them. Fourteen disappearances were being investigated. Six victims were found dead and turned up in various locations throughout the city.

One was a woman, 52 years old, her name was Lois Fidler. The flu didn't kill her. She had been stabbed 48 times, and the odd thing about her death was that part of her hair was chopped off. The second victim was a man, Bill Layton, age 57, who was coming home from work. He routinely took a shortcut that took him across railroad tracks. This is where his body was found, he had been stabbed 14 times. It appeared that he was missing a lock of hair. The third victim was Alice Reading, 16; she was on the way home from school. She had been stabbed six times and a portion of her hair was missing. The fourth and fifth victims were sisters, Crystal and Charlotte Tomlinson, ages 6, and 7, each had been stabbed 10 times and each had their hair cut. The sixth and final victim that they found was a 72-year-old man named Ralph Waters. He had been found in a field just outside of the Chicago proper. He was stabbed just once in the heart. The man was bald so no hair was taken.

Whoever the killer was remained a deep mystery because there were very little clues left at any of the scenes. The additional eight disappearances were still in question. All of these headlines had been in the newspapers for the last several weeks, but today the headlines held a different death message.

CITYWIDE FLU HITS CHICAGO. CITY IS SHUTTING DOWN.

The entire city of Chicago has been advised to stay indoors because the continuing widespread cases of the flu. Health officials advise against going into any public places.

The article went on to read more about precautions everyone should take to help stop the flow of the flu epidemic. The worst was yet to come.

8

It was almost two weeks and the flu epidemic continued to rage on, but that did not stop Jaden and Lise from going to work. Jaden worked with the sanitary department and his role in this ongoing crisis was imperative. Lise continued on in the hated position on the assembly line. The company was too greedy to close their doors and insisted that their workers continue on a daily basis. That left Molly and Gunda to take care of the other children.

Molly put a cup of porridge in front of Mable. She pushed it away. "Eat it."

Gunda sat down next to Mable. "She needs a little help." She took the spoon and made sure the food wasn't too hot before she offered it to her sister. Mable pushed the spoon away.

"Just look at them. All three of them. We have to feed them and none of them want to eat."

"Do you really expect James to feed himself?"

Just as the discussion was getting heated between the two sisters Lise came into the apartment. Molly knew immediately that she had been drinking.

"Mother! You're drunk."

"So what." She spat. "I went to that stupid job and stayed there all day. It's after five and I need a reward. I deserve it. Get the hell away from me."

That was the moment Mable decided to turn over her porridge bowl and start to cry which set James off and he started to cry even harder.

"Shut them up." Lise screamed and grabbed her head.

Gunda quickly placed James in the broken crib and then took Mable and put her next to him. She put some milk in a pan and warmed it. She went and got the two bottles rinse them out and poured milk into them. All the time she was doing this Lise continued to scream at Molly. Molly in turn was screaming back at her. Both Mable and James were crying.

"Willie's sick." Molly yelled. "Really sick. He needs his mother and look at you."

"Tell Gunda to take care of the little whiner."

When Gunda finished filling the two bottles with milk she went over to the crib and gave one to each baby. They started to drink and became quiet for which she was grateful, it was a relief. Between Lise's and Molly's screaming and the two babies crying she almost screamed herself. Michael sat at the kitchen table with his porridge in front of him and said nothing. He looked like a small statue holding a spoon in its hand. The only other one who was really quiet was Willie.

Lise walked away from Molly after screaming she should mind her own damn business before she slapped her silly. When she was done with her sister she turned on Gunda.

Though gritted teeth Lise spit. "YOU. Get yourself over to that store and get me my medicine."

Lise threw $.50 at Gunda and marched over to her bedroom slamming the door. Molly and Gunda just stood looking at each other.

"You'd better go, or she'll just get worse."

"Okay Molly, I'll hurry back. I hope John Poll is feeling better."

Gunda didn't bother with the wagon this time because all she was going to get was the bottle for her mother. She ran most of the way to Shadowland Groceries stopping only once to catch her breath. When she got there she stopped abruptly at the door. It was locked. She couldn't remember it ever being locked. There was a note on the door which read:

Closed due to death in family

Gunda wondered who had died in John Poll's family. She knew that he had a brother and a sister so maybe one of them had passed. She slowly walked back to the apartment. On the way she noticed that few people were on the streets, and it was always seemed crowded. The drugstore on the corner was dark and had a closed sign on it. Even the Five and Dime was locked and had a closed sign. She wondered if it was a holiday she didn't know about or maybe it was because people were getting sick. She had read something about that in the paper.

She slowly walked from street to street finding only a few people. They would cross the street to avoid her and she wondered why. The wind had picked up and it was getting colder again so she hurried towards home. On the way she leaned down and picked up a piece of newspaper that caught on her leg. She started to pick up more newspapers. It would give her something to read to the other children.

She was crushing newspapers to her chest when she saw one of her neighbors, Mr. Phil Watson walking down the street towards her. When he came closer she called out to him. "Hi, Mr. Watson."

She thought it was strange that he didn't answer her and just continued to walk in a straight line that took him into the street. She ran after him and grabbed his hand pulling him back onto the sidewalk. "You're going to get hit if a car comes along."

He didn't answer her and staggered down the sidewalk talking, but there was no one to talk to. She watched him for a few minutes before she turned back to go home.

When she got there Gunda climbed the stairs up to the third floor. She went in and found her father sitting at the kitchen table with his head in his hands. She took a step toward him when she heard Molly calling to her.

She looked over to where Molly was standing, she was gesturing to her. When she got close enough she grabbed her arm and pulled her into their bedroom. Michael was sitting quietly on the bed.

"What happened?"

"Shhh. Come over here."

Gunda thought that Molly was not only acting strange, but she seemed nervous." What's wrong?"

"William's really sick."

"I know that."

"They sent someone here."

"Who?"

"Some nurse from the health department. She's in with William now."

Gunda walked out of the bedroom and went over to the kitchen where her father was still sitting at the table. "Who is that woman?"

"She's from the city Board of Health. They think that William has a disease that can spread to other people."

"Willie hasn't been by other people except Nicholas downstairs. Is he sick too?"

"I don't know."

The nurse walked out of William's bedroom and asked Jaden how long William was sick. Jaden turned to Gunda.

"Maybe two or three days ago. He got really hot."

"I want you to pay careful attention to me because I'm going to tell you what to do to protect yourselves. I will not repeat this so you must listen intently. This flu is very bad and you must all take precautions. If you have masks I suggest you wear them. Avoid crowds and people who appear sick.

You, girl, open all the windows and air out the apartment. Breathe deeply of the fresh air; it will help clear your lungs. Clean this apartment from top to bottom. Make sure you wash your hands carefully and often."

"How sick is Willie?"

"He has the flu."

"When will he get better?"

"That remains to be seen."

"Willie was playing with Nicholas downstairs. I don't know if he sick or not."

"I will check on him before leave."

Nicholas Price, age 6, died that night of the flu. The rest of his family was also sick with the flu. They would all die within days.

~ ~ ~

The next morning Lise told all of them to go to school and that she would be home with Mable, Michael, and Jimmy.

"What about Willie? That nurse said we were supposed to stay home."

"Go to school? Get out! Now!"

The weather had turned even colder and both Gunda and Molly slipped into the new coats that Jaden had brought home. They quietly left the house so they wouldn't disturb Lise.

On the way Gunda saw something lying in the gutter. It looked brown, furry, and soft. The cold rain from last night had soaked it through. She thought maybe it was a dog or cat. She went over to investigate and discovered a ratty looking teddy bear. It had soaked up the water and dirt from the gutter. She picked it up and shook it.

"Put that nasty thing back in the gutter."

Gunda squeezed out as much of the water from the teddy as she could and ran to catch up to Molly. She looked at the teddy bear in her hand and said, "What is that nasty thing?"

"A teddy bear. I'm going to clean him up and give him to Willie."

Molly took the teddy bear from Gunda and looked at it critically. It was a dirty mess and had a ripped arm and only one eye because the button was missing for the other one.

She shoved it back at her. "If you insist on keeping it you carry it."

When they got to the school they were surprised to find it was still open. With the continuing problems of the flu, there was speculation whether or not the school would be closed. It seemed like every family had someone sick.

"I thought it would be closed."

"Who knows? Let's go in Gunda."

The halls were mostly empty. Few students were in the classrooms. Molly's friend, Sarah Turcio stopped her as she was entering her class. They talked for a few minutes and together decided to leave school and go to Sarah's house. Her parents were both working and her brother was at school. When they entered her house everything seemed unusually quiet.

"Do you want a cup of coffee?"

Molly had never tasted coffee before, but didn't want Sarah to know that she had no clue what it would taste like so she said yes. They sat at the kitchen table together with the coffee between them. Molly was surprised at the taste and decided right away that she actually liked it.

"This is really good."

"It's okay. Did you hear about Henry?"

"Henry Mandy?"

"That's the one. He's been really sick. Out of his mind sick. His mother when running in the streets last night screaming how her boy was dying."

Molly felt fear gripped her and decided that she had to go to him immediately. "

"Thanks Sarah. I have to go."

"Go where?"

"I have to see Henry."

Molly ran most of the way to Henry's house. When she got there she stood on the doorstep trying to catch her breath and then rang the bell. When no one answered she tried the door. She was surprised to find it open. She walked through the house calling Henry's name.

She heard a groan from the room toward the back of the house. She followed the corridor back to a bedroom where she found Henry laying on the couch wrapped in a blanket.

She went over and took his hand; she was alarmed at how hot he felt. "Henry."

When Henry opened his eyes she could see that they were filled with fever. He was looking at her, but not really seeing her.

"Don't die, Henry." Molly said in desperation. "I need your help. The baby."

"Molly?"

"It's me. What can I do to help you?"

"Nothing. I'm dying. I got that flu."

"No. You'll be all right. You have to be. I need you. Your baby, our baby needs you."

"Baby? No. No, not me."

"It is your baby, but don't talk now. Let me get a cool cloth for your head."

There was noise from the doorway and a high shrill voice said, "Who the hell are you?"

Molly abruptly stood up. She glanced down at Henry and then stammered, "I........ Molly. Henry and I are friends."

"And you think that that kid you're cooking is his?"

"I didn't know you heard me. Yes, the baby is Henry's."

"Not in this lifetime, little girl. Henry don't have a kid, yours or anyone else's. Get out."

"Mrs. Mandy if you..."

"Shut up. Can't you see how sick Henry is and you're coming around here accusing him of knocking you up. My Henry isn't that kind, get out."

"Alright I'll go, but please let me know how Henry is doing?"

Molly turned to Henry and lightly touched his head before taking his hand.

Henry briefly rose up before he took his last breath. She felt the life leave his body. She dropped his hand and stepped back abruptly. She shook her head and cried, "No."

Hot tears filled her eyes as she ran down the hallway and out into the street. Behind her she heard Henry's mother scream. She became so panicked and frightened all she could think to do was run. When she got home she sprinted up the three flights of stairs and burst through the door calling for her mother. There was no answer. She called again. Michael walked out of the bedroom and over to Molly. He took her hand and led her to where Mable was laying on the floor fast asleep. He pointed at his sister. "Mable."

Molly wiped her tears from her eyes and picked up her little sister carrying her to the bedroom and gently laying her on the bed. She turned to Michael, "go get mother."

"Can't. She went away."

"Away where?"

The little boy shrugged his head and said, "Don't know. Just away."

~~~

When Gunda got home Molly told her she thought Mable may also be sick. Gunda went in and shook her little sister Mable who looked up at her with great big blue eyes and said, "Hi."

Gunda grinned at her. "Hi." She touched her arm and was relieved that she wasn't hot. "Go back to sleep."

"Kay."
~~~

Gunda went back to Molly and said, "I think she's okay. She's not hot."

She noticed that Molly had been crying. She went over and put her hand on her shoulder and asked what was wrong. Molly went into the kitchen and sat down heavily on to a chair.

"I lost my friend today. Henry. He died from the flu."

"Did you touch him?"

"Yes."

"You need to wash. The nurse lady who was here said so."

"He's dead Gunda. I'll never see him again, never talk to him. I loved him so."

"You're only 14, how can you love him?"

"I just do. One day you'll understand."

9

The Newspaper headlines screamed:

<u>Serial Killer Still Haunts Chicago as Flu</u>

<u>Rages on</u>

Chicago and much of the nation are gripped in the worst flu epidemic known to the world. People continue to die at an alarming rate. There is nowhere that is safe and nowhere to hide from this deadly disease. Health organizations continue to fight while the public dies. Chicago is coming to a slow halt as the disease rages through the city. The entire world is affected with closures all over the globe.

The deadly flu is not the only killer that is among us. Three more young girls, Helen Staple, age 9, Lillian Smart, age 11, and Catherine Long, age 6 have seemingly disappeared. All three girls are blonde haired and blue-eyed. They were last seen leaving State and Lake, they never reached home. They started questioning friends and neighbors, but as of today their whereabouts remain unknown.

A fourth girl, Martha Mitchell, age 8 was found dead near Kimball and Levitt in a grassy field. She had been stabbed six times. Anyone with knowledge of these crimes is asked to call the police department.

The boy read the article for the third time and smiled. He carefully cut it out of the paper and pulled a book off of his shelf. He opened it and folded the article into one of the pages. He had 10 articles hidden in this book. Everyone referred to him as the serial killer which made him laugh. He loved the name. He knew that he had them all fooled. No one knew who he really was. He was a good-looking boy, average height and generally fit into any situation. He dressed well and was polite to everyone. You could be standing right next to him and never know that he was the serial killer that everyone was looking for. They didn't know that when he was 10 years old he had randomly killed an eight-year-old that he had lured to the Cumberland forest preserve at Irving and Cumberland. They had walked deep into the preserve and into an isolated area. He waited until Al Reads had his back to him and picked up a large rock. He smashed him in the head with it.

The boy killer had learned a valuable lesson that day because the other kid, Al Reads went down, but was not dead. He got up and attempted to run but had been too stunned to get far. The killer caught up with him and easily hit him again with another rock. This time the kid didn't get up. Just to make sure that he was dead the boy killer continued to hit him until blood flowed freely from his nose, ears and head. It was his first kill.

Once he was dead he buried him underneath a pile of rocks. He had gathered enough to completely cover the corpse and laughed while he did it.

The following day the boy killer snuck out of his house and went down to a variety store that sold used goods. He didn't hesitate and broke in. It was easy. He had checked out the store to see what he needed. He had spent hours to searching through the store.

It was a large store and consisted of three rooms that were attached and flowed into each other. One room had everything that would be needed for the house. From pots and pans to stoves. You could buy materials, paper goods, cups, plates, silverware, curtains, dish towels, soaps and general household goods.

The second room was filled with different types of clothing. Ladies wear, men's, children's and babies. There was a small area that was dedicated to undergarments and accessories. Hats, coats, and scarves were also available for purchase.

The third room was where Guns of all sorts and ammunition were purchased. There were knives of every variety and even bows and arrows could be bought. Hunting gear, tents, and outdoor equipment were also in this room. There were hunting jackets for those who could afford the luxury. This was the room where the boy killer searched. He went directly to the counter where he could find what he needed. He didn't want to spend any more time than necessary in the store so he grabbed everything in the display counter and shoved it into a bag he had picked up in the store. He left as quietly as he had gone in.

Once the boy killer got home he dumped the entire bag of knives on his bed. There were six of various sizes and lengths. He sat on the bed and lovingly caressed each one. He loved the way they shined, the sharpness of the blades, but what he loved the best about his new found friends is what they could do.

His second kill was a seven-year-old girl named Elizabeth Hampton. She went to his school and was a nasty little kid who made fun of him every chance she got. She would point to him in the school yard and call him fatty. That was two years ago and he was no longer fat. He also was no longer timid. He showed no fear or a lack of confidence. He could kill with no conscience.

He went into his closet pulled on a pair of black pants and a black shirt. There was an old dresser in the back of the closet. Getting down on his knees he opened the bottom drawer and inside he found his six friends waiting for him. He had carefully cleaned and sharpened each one. He pulled out the one with the brown handle and lovingly held it in his hands. He closed his eyes and took several deep breaths. This was his favorite. He laughed and thought that it was time for him to go out and have some fun.

~ ~ ~

When Gunda got home she took the teddy bear and scrubbed him until he was clean. It took several soaping's and rinsing's before she was satisfied. After the bear smelled better she placed him in the bathtub to dry and then went to check on Willie.

Lise was supposed to be home, but was gone again. Molly was furious. Now both William and Mable were sick and she didn't know what to do about it. She was still anxious and uneasy over Henry's death and here she was with two sick little kids and no one to turn to. She walked into William room and saw Gunda struggling to pull a blanket over both him and Mable. The blanket was too small.

William and Mable were both shaking with chills that continue to attack them. They were both hot to the touch and whimpering. They seemed to sleep a lot, but she didn't know if that was a good thing. Gunda got her red coat and covered Mable with it. Molly covered William with the blanket.

The two sisters went out to the kitchen and sat down at the table. They were discussing what they thought could be done for Willie and Mable when Molly suddenly started to cry which alarmed to Gunda. She got up went over and put her arms around Molly.

"Everything is so screwed up." Molly cried. "Gunda, I'm leaving."

Nothing could've shocked her more than that statement. "Where are you going?" She stammered.

"It doesn't matter."

Gunda noticed the suitcase by the door for the first time. She went over and tapped it. "It's late. You're taking a suitcase? Where do you think you're going?"

"Come on out in the hall."

They went out onto the landing and sat down on the top step that led down to the hallway and front door.

"I'm leaving tonight."

"And where are you going? That's crazy Molly."

"I don't know where, but I'll send you a letter to let you know where I am."

"You can't. It's dark and everyone in the city is sick. Everyone in the whole world is sick. There's nowhere for you to go."

"Keep your voice down. I don't want anyone to hear us."

"Why? Jaden not here, he's at work, and Lise is dead drunk. The building could come down around her and she wouldn't even hear it."

"I have to go. You don't understand. I can't let them know. Jaden will kill me if he finds out."

"Finds out what? You can't go. You can't be alone. You need to stay here with us."

"I'm going to………. Lise, she won't care. She'll just call me a slut and constantly remind me what a stupid kid I am."

"Molly, what you're talking about. Why would she call you a slut?"

Molly picked up the suitcase, took Gunda's hand and went into the kitchen. They sat down at the table. She slowly nodded her head, "If I tell you secret can you keep it to yourself?"

"Of course."

You can't tell Lise or Jaden. Not ever."

"Okay. I promise."

"You have to give me your most solemn promise."

Gunda crossed her heart and said, "I won't tell. I won't ever tell. Cross my heart."

Molly decided to just blurt it out. "I'm pregnant."

Gunda couldn't say anything. She didn't know what to say. Finally she spit out, "Why?"

Molly got up so fast from the chair that it tipped over. "What do you mean why? It happened that's why."

"Is Henry the father?"

"Yeah. Henry's the father alright."

"But you're only 14. How old is he?"

"He'll always be 17. Henry is dead."

Gunda sat staring at Molly. "We can work this out."

"I can't. You know how nasty Lise is."

"Molly, you just can't leave what if something happens to you? What if you need help with the baby? I'll help you."

She gave Gunda a sad smile. "Everything seems to fall to you, you've got enough to do."

"And I need your help. I can't do it alone. I don't know what to do. The kids are sick. Mother is a drunk who can't be counted on for anything. Just look at the garbage she gives us to eat. I am so sick of porridge every day. And Jaden, he's never here. I love you Molly. I'm afraid. We have to stick together. If you leave with what's going on, you may die."

Molly thought about her situation. She signed. "I'll stay. You're right, I don't know why I thought that running would help. There's no way I can run from this. This baby is mine and he, or she will be a part of this family. I just wish that Jaden would be here more."

"He has to work." Gunda said in a tiny voice. "He can't help it he's not here."

"Yeah, well, he closes his eyes to a lot of what's going on."

Before they could continue the conversation Willie started yelling which woke Mable and made her start crying.

"Great!" Molly yelled.

"Maybe we should get a doctor for them."

"With what? We have no money."

"I have $6.33."

"Where did you get money?"

Before Gunda could answer there was another scream from Willie. "It doesn't matter." Molly said.

Gunda looked over at the bedroom. "Let's make some bottles for them, maybe it will calm them down."

They made three bottles, one for Willie, one for Mable, and one for James. She brought them to Molly. "We're out of milk and porridge. I'm going to go to Shadowland Groceries. Molly, are you sure you're going to have a baby?"

Molly leaned against the doorway and sighed. "Positive."

"Why don't you tell father?"

"No. Let's talk about it later. You go get some food. Here, I found a dollar in Jaden's dresser. If Shadowland is closed you'll have to go over to Zion's."

"That's over a mile."

"It can't be helped. Take the wagon."

Gunda noticed that Molly never called their parents mother and father anymore. Even she had started calling her mother, Lise." Maybe we should put Mable in our room in case Willie's got something that's really catching."

"He has the flu and she probably has it if he does, but I'll put her in our room. You go. I'll take care of it."

Gunda took the dollar and went downstairs for the wagon. The apartment's front door was what they called a double. There were actually two doors and both of them had heavy glass inserts. The inner one had a lock long ago, but it's been broken for years. As she turned to duck under the stairs to get the wagon a shadow from the outside door fell over her. She froze and watched as it came closer. It completely engulfed her; she got scared and dove under the staircase.

She crawled into the wagon and covered her eyes. She heard the inner door open with its distinctive squeak. She remained as still as possible slapping her hands over her mouth so she wouldn't make any noise.

She couldn't explain why the shadow frightened her, but somehow she knew that it was filled with evil. The shadow walked by her without stopping. She took a deep breath and held it. Ten minutes later when she heard nothing and saw nothing so she cautiously got out of the wagon and looked down the hall both ways. No one was there. She quickly pulled the wagon out and ran all the way to the next block with it. Gunda continued to look behind her for someone who might be following, but there was no one there. It looked like there was no one anywhere. The street was deserted. She shrugged and continued to Mr. Poll's.

~~~
~~~

The boy killer knew that Gunda was under the stairs, but she wasn't his target. The target was actually his father. He laughed thinking that his wonderful father was living on borrowed time. He hated him.

The boy killer was out of school because of the whole flu thing. Yesterday his old man had come home in a foul mood; the factory he was working in was closing at the end of the week because of the flu epidemic. He took it out on him. He still had the bruises from his foul mood.

Chris Bounce worked at the same factory as Lise. They worked side-by-side on the same assembly line and became friendly over the last few weeks. They spent all of their free time together even sharing their lunches. After about a month they were lovers. He didn't really care about her, but she was good in bed.

Lise found Chris exciting where Jaden was boring. He lavished her with the attention that Jaden had never done. The problem as she saw it was that they were both married and both had children.

Chris had a wife, Elizabeth, and twin sons, Brian and Elton, age 15. To further complicate things after three months together Lise discovered that she was pregnant. They were lying together in bed at Chris's house when he suggested she tell Jaden it was his baby. She shook her head and kissed him. His wife was at work and the boys were at school. What they didn't know was that the school had closed today and they were sending all the children home.

"I'm telling you, if you need to tell old Jaden he has another bundle of joy coming."

"I can't. We haven't been together in months. The baby is definitely yours and I can't do this alone."

"This is a problem, Lise because I can't leave my wife and sons. They won't survive without me."

"What are we going to do about it?"

"Let me think about it maybe I can come up with something."

"You'd better think fast."

Chris heard the front door open and put his finger to his lips. "Stay here." He whispered.

He quickly stepped into his pants and threw on his shirt. "Be quiet."

Chris nonchalantly strolled out into the living room where he found Elton. "Why aren't you in school?"

"They let us out because of the flu thing."

"Where's your brother?"

"I don't know. What are you doing home at this time a day dad?"

"I wasn't feeling well and came home."

Lise could hear Chris speaking to someone. She knew it wasn't his wife because the voice was deeper than a woman's. She pulled on her dress and grabbed her purse. She decided her best option was to go out the window. Fortunately, Chris lived on the first floor and it was only a short drop to the ground. When she made it out the window she went over to Otto Meshes bar for a drink. She needed one desperately. She also needed time to think about her situation and what the best way to solve it was. Right now the best way for her was a nice, cool, dark bar.

~~~

Gunda stood in front of Shadowland Grocery store and stared at the same notice that she had seen before. She knew she couldn't go home without some food because there was no more in the
~~~

apartment. It seemed like she was always hungry and there was never enough food.

Gunda pulled the wagon behind her as she started out for Zion's market a good mile away. She turned to the right to go through the park because it would be shorter. As she walked through Horner Park she again wondered if John Poll was the person in the death notice on the door.

The park was so quiet that she turned around to see if there was anyone else there. There was no activity anywhere, no children were playing, and no adults were walking dogs, there was no one around. It was almost like an empty city of its very own. The streets were deserted as she went down them. She found it strange and somehow frightening at the same time. Where the streets were once busy with activity everything now seemed deserted. She felt like she may be the only person left in the entire world.

Suddenly the park that she knew so well and had played in all her life no longer seem to be her friend, but something to fear. The cold wind pushed at her back hurrying her along. She couldn't wait to leave.

Gunda exited the park and began to feel a little better as she hurried along to Zion market. She left her wagon outside of the market. It was a much bigger store than the Shadowland Market. She didn't know where to find anything so she started down the first aisle. There were food items she didn't know and had never seen before. She picked up a chocolate bar and lifted it to her nose. She took a deep breath and smelled the wonderful aroma of the chocolate. She didn't remember ever having a chocolate bar and knew she wouldn't be having it today. There was no money for it. She gently put it back down on the shelf. She looked down the long aisle and saw no one. She grabbed the chocolate bar and stuffed it down her shirt.

After searching most of the aisles she felt she had all the groceries she needed and started to the checkout counter. At the last minute Gunda added a bottle of aspirin. If she could get Willie to take it maybe it would help the fever go away.

She was in the last aisle when a young boy came over to talk to her.

"You better hurry up because we're closing in a few minutes."

"For good?"

"I don't think so. Probably just until this flu thing gets done. Mr. Morton said you should hurry and get out, so finish up and don't bother coming back here for a long while."

"I won't be long."

Gunda quickly scanned the shelves for more groceries. She picked up more of the hated porridge and added it to her wagon. She knew she'd need milk, and left the cart to run back to the first aisle where she thought she saw it. Now she was ready to leave and retrieved the wagon from outside and hurried to the counter to check out.

"It's about time, everyone else has left." The same boy said to her.

Gunda heard the lock click behind her after she was almost shoved out the door.

10

Jaden came in with three blankets under his arm. He handed them to Molly. She looked at them curiously and asked, "Where did you get them?"

"Never mind. There's one for each bed. It's getting colder at night. Where is everyone?"

"William's in bed because he's still sick. James is in his crib sleeping. Michael is sleeping in our room with Mable."

Michael jumped out from behind the couch. Raised his arms high in the air and yelled, "I'm here."

"Where's Gunda?"

"She went for groceries. She should be back really soon."

Ten minutes later Gunda pushed open the door. She had her arms full with part of the groceries. It was all she could carry up by herself. Jaden took them from her and went downstairs to help her bring up the rest. When they were all on the table Jaden looked at them carefully and asked, "Is this all of it?"

"Yes father."

"Is this what you always eat? I give mother enough money for more. Where are the potatoes, and maybe a little meat for the pot?"

"There isn't enough money for meat."

"How much did Lise give you?"

"A little over a dollar."

Jaden was furious. "The booze." He knew that she was buying booze instead of food for the children. He should have known that was where she got the money for it but he had been so busy working he didn't notice.

"Where is your mother?"

Gunda shrugged. "At work?"

~~~

Jaden stayed up and waited for Lise to come home. It was late and all of the children had gone to bed. Lise came staggering through the door and almost fell. She giggled hysterically slapping her hand over her mouth. It was after one in the morning. Jaden had been sitting quietly in the dark at the kitchen table. He turned and looked at her.

"You're drunk."

Lise was surprised when she heard Jaden's voice. "Jaden?"

"Who else did you expect?"

"Where are the kids?"

"Sleeping. Something that you would know if you'd been here. It's late. Where have you been?"

"I was at the crappy job your forcing me to go to and then I stopped for a glass of beer."

"I'm sure you drink more than one glass of beer."

Lise straightened and tried to look dignified and sober as she walked further into the kitchen. "One drink Jaden. One! I deserve it after a long day in that sweatshop."

Jaden tried to quell his anger as he got up and stepped towards her. "What have you been doing with the money I give you to buy food for the children?"
~~~

Lise took a step back from Jaden. "What are you talking about? They eat."

"Milk and porridge. That's it. I give you enough money to do better than that. I know that you're drinking instead of buying food for them."

Gunda and Molly listened to them argue until they stomped down the hall to their bedroom. Now all they could hear were muffled voices.

"All they do is fight."

"Father's angry about the food."

"You shouldn't have told him about it."

"I didn't. He saw what was there. You better not tell him about the baby. Not while he's this mad."

"I don't plan on it. I think I'm going to get rid of it."

"How do you do that?"

"You go to a Doctor and he takes it out, but it costs a lot of money."

"If they give the baby to some nice people maybe they will pay for it."

Molly realized that Gunda didn't understand that she was talking about aborting the baby. She could see no other option. She was only 14 and couldn't even get a job. She didn't want to face what her mother and father would do and say if they knew. She couldn't even run away because there was nowhere to go. She would have to find out where she could go for an abortion and how much it would cost.

"Go to sleep Gunda."

~~~

Jaden left early the next morning, but before he left he went to talk to Gunda. He gave her three dollars. "Keep this in case you need money for food. Hide it from your mother or she will buy.................." he stopped short of saying the word booze.

"Whiskey?"

It saddened Jaden that his 8 year old daughter knew about Lise. "Yes Gunda. Whiskey."

"I'll hide it well, Father. Lise won't find it."

Jaden leaned down and kissed Gunda's forehead and then he was gone. Gunda couldn't sleep after father had left. She lay in the bed wide awake thinking about their short conversation. He knew about Lise. All this time he knew. He had turned away from her mother's problem until he no longer could. Maybe now things would be easier, but somehow she doubted it.

Gunda got up and started the porridge. James, Mable, and Michael will get up early and they would all be hungry. She also had to work on Willie and see if she could get him to eat. She had to push the chair up to the stove to be tall enough to reach it and stir the pot.

While the porridge was cooling she went to check on Willie. The little boy was lying on his side with his face to the wall. She called to him, but he didn't respond. She turned him over and was shocked to find his face beet red with a bluish tinge.

Gunda ran to get her mother. She shook her hard and called her name, but Lise just rolled over and told her to get away from her.

"Mother, Willie's really sick. Mother!!!"

"I'm sick. Go way."
~~~

Gunda went back to the kitchen and filled a pan with cool water. She put rags across Willie's chest, arms, and legs. She shook him slightly. "Willie can you hear me?" What she didn't know was that Willie was in a coma and wouldn't be talking to anyone ever again.

Molly had run all the way to the Board of Health to get help for Willie. They said a nurse would come and that she should go back home. It was almost four hours until the nurse came to see Willie. It was too late.

The nurse came out and verified that Willie had died of the Spanish flu. Before he had gone into a coma he had developed severe pneumonia. That resulted in the bluish color and the dark spots that appeared on his face. It actually suffocated him as his lungs failed from the lack of oxygen. His lungs had filled with a frothy, bloody liquid that caused his death.

Gunda bolted from the kitchen and went into Willie's room. He looked like he was sleeping. She approached him very slowly and took his hand in hers. She felt the coldness that was there and stood for a long time just watching him, willing him to come back to life. She was still sitting with Willie when the health nurse told her to get out and to make sure she washed her hands.

She stood next to Molly, "I knew Willie was sick, but I didn't think he was going to die." Gunda said sadly with tears flowing down her cheeks.

"I did the best I could."

"It wasn't your fault. Mother should have been here to take care of Willie. It was her responsibility. Maybe Willie would still be alive if she took better care of him."

The two sisters held onto each other as they spoke quietly about the brother they had just lost. Gunda would never understand how her mother could lay up in the bed drunk and let little Willie die like that. She knew that she would always miss him.

After Willie was removed to the local funeral home, Jaden told everyone to go to bed. He didn't want to discuss Willie and would only say that nothing else could be done for him.

11

Gunda was holding the tattered little bear in her hands. It had once been a bright green, but now was nothing more than a pale green color. She had wanted to give it to Willie to keep him company while he was sick, but Willie was gone from her forever and she never got to give him the sad little bear. Mable who had been sick was doing much better; she paddled into the room on bare feet and pointed at the bear. Gunda smiled at her and handed the bear to her. She giggled.

"It's a bear."

"Bear." Mable repeated the word and sat down on the floor. She held the bear out at arm's length and said, "Bear."

Gunda leaned down so she was looking right into her face. "That's right, it's a bear."

Mable hugged the little bear to her and then placed it on the floor. She laid across the bears belly and put her thumb in her mouth before going to sleep. Gunda placed one of the new blankets across her.

~~~

Gunda sat next to the window looking out. It seemed like the entire city of Chicago had come to a stop. The trains were no longer running. Cars no longer drove down the street and even the horse carts were gone. There were no people at all. Even the children she was used to seeing were gone.

"It's like no one lives here anymore." She whispered.

Molly came up behind her and said, "I'm sick. I think I got Willie's flu."

~~~

Father came home that night exhausted. He had been assigned to the crews attempting to remove and bury the dead. It was hard and depressing work because there was no shortage of bodies. Sometimes they would find whole families dead in their homes. They would be just lying in their beds like they were sleeping, but there was always the telltale smell of death surrounding them.

Caskets were sitting in rooms waiting for burial. They would find the dead lined up in the streets or propped up on curbs against buildings. It seemed like the entire city had been indurated with dead people, they were everywhere. There were not enough people to bury them.

Jaden had taken his son, Willie to be buried. Right now there was a severe back up because the grave diggers couldn't keep up. Jaden's friend, Bert Carsten was one of the grave diggers and he said he would personally take care of Willie. He wrapped the little body in a blanket gently laying him down to rest.

Willie had no coffin because they had run out of them days before and the coffin makers couldn't keep up with the demand. The dead were being buried in mass graves. Heavy equipment was brought into the Taylor Memorial Center where several sites were designated for the mass graves. Bert made sure that Willie was buried alone, in the back of the cemetery under a shade tree. He personally dug the grave and laid the little boy to rest.

~ ~ ~

There was a knock at the door. Gunda opened it to find two women standing there. They both had on long black dresses and had gloves on their hands. They were delivering soup to the homes of ill families. She asked if they wanted to come in but they declined. She thanked them for the soup and they left immediately. She took the soup into the kitchen and set it on the stove. It smelled good. She got a spoon and tasted the soup and smiled, it was good and a relief from the daily porridge she had had for the last few months.

Lise dragged herself through the door; it banged against the wall as she staggered into the room. Gunda watched her weave her way over to the stove, she seemed to be walking with great difficulty.

"What is this crap and where did it come from?"

"It's soup, Lise. It's really good and I'm going to warm some up for Molly."

Gunda wondered when she had started calling her mother by her first name. It really didn't matter because she hasn't really been a mother to them in a long time. Lise didn't even seem to know that she didn't call her mother. She watched as Lise weaved down the hallway and into her bedroom. Several minutes later she reappeared and walked to the front door that was still open.

"I'm going out."

"But everyone is sick. Even James's is burning with the fever. They want you to take care of them. I need your help."

Lise completely ignored Gunda and slammed the door as she left. Gunda slowly eased down into a chair next to the kitchen table. Everyone was sick and she wasn't sure she knew what to do. She put her head on the table and started to cry. A few minutes later, she pushed herself up and went to check on everyone and was relieved that they were all sleeping. She went over to the stove and turned off the soup. She would save it for later. Gunda wanted to cry again, she had never felt so alone.

Father worked so much that he wasn't home to help her and when he was home he was so tired all he managed to do was eat something and then go to bed.

It was getting dark outside as the day was going away from them. She collected some papers from the street last week but hadn't had a chance to look at them. She laid the papers out on the table. Most of the articles in the paper were about how horrible the current flu was in the city of Chicago. There was one about 14 famous people who had the flu and survived it. As she read the list the name she recognized a few of them. Among the survivors was a young man named Walt Disney. Franklin D Roosevelt, Woodrow Wilson and Mary Pickford who she knew was a silent movie star.

She immediately recognized the name of Ernest H Miles. He was the Prime Minister of the United Kingdom, she had read about him in school. The only other name on the list she knew was Woodrow Wilson, the president. The rest of the people she didn't know.

Gunda stopped reading the paper and pushed it away from her. She started to think about Lise. She decided that she would no longer continue to think of her as part of the family. The startling truth about that hit her hard. Lise was just someone who lived here. She barely talked to them anymore and when she did it was to scream at them. She had even hit Gunda on several occasions. She never cooked a meal, hugged one of her children, or acknowledged them. She didn't care that they were all sick, or that Willie had died. She never even asked about him.

Gunda was tired, tired of everything. She had been up most of the night with James who didn't seem to be able to keep from coughing. She was an eight-year-old child and was now bearing the horrible responsibility of taking care of four of her siblings who were all sick with the flu. Flu that killed. She hadn't slept all night and didn't know how much longer she could do this. She laid her head on the kitchen table and was instantly asleep.

~~~

Lise went downstairs to Chris's apartment and banged on the door. His wife, Elizabeth answered. She stood in the doorway and looked at the disheveled person before her.

"Can I help you?"

"No. Is Chris here?"

"No, he's out. What is it that you want?"

From behind her Brian said, "Yeah. What the hell do you want?"

"Shut up Brian."

Lise decided she better not fight with this woman. She wasn't sure whether or not Elizabeth knew about her and Chris. "My husband isn't home. My daughter's door on her bedroom fell in. I thought Chris could look at it."

"I'll tell him." Elizabeth said and slammed the door in her face. As Lise turned to leave she heard Chris's voice, he was arguing with Elizabeth.

She shrugged and went off to another local bar called Waterman's. Jaden didn't know about this one so she didn't have to worry about him finding her. It was the bar where she and Chris originally met each other.

~~~

The knock on the door woke Gunda up. She went over and stared at the door trying to decide if she should answer it or not. There was a second louder knock. She slowly opened the door and looked out. She wondered if it was another soup woman.

"Hi there."

Gunda looked up at a tall man with a big smile. He was beautiful with soft Brown hair that flow down to his shoulders. His brown eyes twinkled when he smiled at her.

"Hi."

"I'm Eddie Conner's a friend of your father. He asked me to come and help you with your brothers and sisters."

"I don't think I know you."

"You were very little last time I saw you."

Eddie pulled out a picture from his wallet and handed it to her. She looked carefully at it. She was in the picture and so Eddie and Molly. She couldn't have been more than two years old at the time. She was laughing in the picture and Eddie was holding her.

"I still don't think I remember you."

"You father and I are very good friends and I want to be your friend." He held out his hand. "Let's see what I can do to help you."

"I have to make the babies their bottles. I only have to do two now because Willie passed away. The flu got him." She said quietly.

Eddie was appalled at the conditions in the apartment. He looked around at the mess. Someone, probably Gunda had tried to keep things in order. The first thing he did was to change all the bedding. In baby James crib he used a large towel because there were no sheets for it. Gunda helped him change everyone's clothes. Molly was so sick she couldn't even manage to do that by herself. Gunda helped her into one of Jaden's old shirts while Eddie took care of Michael, Mable, and James. He washed each one of them in cool water to make them more comfortable. Once all the beds were cleaned and everyone was in fresh, clean clothes he helped Gunda with the food.

"We got the soup from a lady. She brought it, but Mable and James can only eat weak porridge."

Eddie held Mable in his arms, rocked her slowly and fed her the bottle with the weak porridge in it. Gunda had crawled into James crib and attempted to get him to eat, but after a half-hour she gave up. She held up the bottle in front of her. "He just can't seem to eat."

"Let me put Mable in bed and we'll see if we can get James eat something."

He carried the little girl into the bedroom and placed her under the covers. He placed the pale green bear next to her and leaned down to give her a gentle kiss on the forehead. She hugged the bear and said pointing to it, "Maggie."

He patted her cheek. "You and Maggie try to get some sleep, little one. Pleasant dreams."

Eddie wrapped James in a blanket and cuddled him in his huge arms. He slowly rocked the fussy baby. Gunda had watched him carefully and was surprised when James quieted. She said, "I think he likes that."

"It's a little trick I learned a long time ago. Babies rest easier when you cuddled them."

"How do you know father?"

"We met a long time ago and have remained friends for many years."

"How come I don't remember you?"

"Like I said you wcrc small the last time you saw me. Your mother asked me not to come back here."

Gunda went over and sat on the edge of the chair, "why would she do that?"

"We didn't exactly get along."

Gunda looked up and Eddie saw tears in her eyes, "I don't exactly get along with mother either."

"It's okay Gunda, not everyone can get along in life."

Eddie continued to rock James as he slipped the bottle into his mouth. The baby started to drink.

Gunda wiped her eyes and tried to smile. "It works."

The door clicked open and Jaden came in. He had two bags of groceries in his arms. Gunda immediately went to help him.

She pointed to Eddie. "Eddie has come to help us. I like him."

"I know, I asked him to come and help you. I forgot to tell you."

"He got James to eat."

Jaden went over and leaned down to look at James. He touched his little foot and smiled. "He feels cooler."

"Father, Molly got sick today."

Jaden went in and check on all of the children. Molly and Michael seem to be the sickest. James seems a little better and Mable said she was "all good and that Maggie was better too."

Jaden sat in the chair next to Eddie. He looked over at Gunda and sighed, "Where's your mother?"

"She got mad this morning and left, and she stayed gone."

"Great." He said in disgust.

Eddie touched Jaden's arm. "Tired?"

"Very. Thank you for coming Eddie."

"You know all you have to do is ask."

12

Chris went over to the Waterman's bar looking for Lise. He found her sitting in the back booth nursing a beer. He sat down next to her and snarled, "Don't talk to my wife. Don't come by the apartment again."

"I'm pregnant and it's yours. We need to talk." She spit back.

"About what? Get rid of it. I'm not leaving Elizabeth and the boys. I don't want another kid and you sure as hell don't need one. It's not like you take care any of your kid's."

"Let Jaden take care of them. I want this baby. It's part of us."

"There is no us anymore. I can't do this anymore, Lise. Elizabeth is getting suspicious."

"Suspicious!" She screamed. "I'll go right over there now and tell her."

Chris grabbed Lise by the front of her dress. "You will not speak to Elizabeth, or my boys. You will not go over there. If you do I'll make sure that you and that thing you're carrying will never be a problem again."

He got up so fast the chair crashed to the ground. He turned back to her and shouted, "We're through." He snorted and barreled out the door.

She calmly sat down in the chair and looked at the closing door. "ASSHOLE."

The boy killer was standing outside the window of the bar watching, and because they were so loud he had heard everything that was said. He grinned. "Soon."

~~~
~~~

When Lise walked into her apartment she found Eddie sitting in Jaden's chair, his eyes closed and cuddling the sleeping James in his arms. She tromped over to him and grabbed the baby from his arms. James immediately woke up and started to scream at the top of his lungs.

Jaden came out from Molly's room where he had been sitting with her. Gunda had also been sitting with Molly and her father; she was really worried about her and wondered if she should tell that she's pregnant. She wanted to, but was afraid of what would happen, especially with Lise. What if they made her move while she was still sick? Molly had said that they would make her leave and Gunda believed it.

Jaden looked at Eddie, then Lise and his screaming son. He knew exactly what happened. He confronted his wife, "what do you think you're doing? Eddie just had him calmed down."

She shoved James into Gunda's arms almost causing her to drop him. He began to scream even louder.

Lise turned to Eddie and pointed at him. "What the hell is he doing here?"

"I asked him to come and help us. Gunda can't do it alone, she's only eight years old and I have to work. You should be here. Where have you been this late?"

"None of your business. I don't have to answer to you anymore."

Eddie got up and took James from Gunda and ushered her into the bedroom. He sat on the bed and slowly rocked the baby until he calmed again. Gunda sat next to him holding onto his arm. Michael looked up from the bed and pointed to the other room.

Gunda went to Michael and smoothed back his hair. "It's okay Michael, just don't listen. Close your eyes and go back to sleep. They're just arguing again."

"Don't leave me, Gunda."

Eddie placed his hand on Michael's cheek. "We'll be right here. Close those beautiful eyes baby and everything will be alright. We won't leave you."

James finally stopped crying. Eddie placed him into the crib and covered him with a blanket. He went back and sat next to Gunda and Michael. They could hear Jaden and Lise continuing their argument. At one point it sounded like Lise threw something at Jaden.

She looked up at Eddie and shrugged, "they do that a lot now, even before everyone got sick."

Eddie put his arm around Gunda and pulled her close to him. "Don't worry. People argue all the time, they get over it."

"She drinks so much and father gets mad. Eddie, will you come back tomorrow. Lise will be gone and father will have to go help bury the dead people." She shook her head. "It seems like everybody is dead."

"Not everyone, sweetheart. It's a bad disease and some people just aren't strong enough to fight it."

"Is that why Willie died? Because he wasn't strong enough?"

"Well now, I think maybe God needed Willie to help him welcome all the others who are going home to heaven."

"Really? You really think that?"

"Yes, Gunda, that's what I believe. Willie had a great smile and he would be perfect for that job."

"When the flu is done and everybody is better can Willie come back?"

"Not anymore Michael, he has to stay and help God with other things."

"You think Willie's happy in heaven?"

Eddie hugged Gunda again. "Everyone is happy in heaven. It's a wonderful place."

Gunda more than liked Eddie, she thought she loved him. He was soft spoken and a great hugger. He never scolded her and he never hit her. He also saw to that there was always something to eat in their house. It seemed like it was the first time she wasn't hungry all the time. She thought about her mother and father. Her mother never hugged her and she barely spoke to her, when she did she wished she hadn't because she always seemed angry. Her father, all he did was work and she barely saw him. He hugged her once in a while. Eddie was like a breath of fresh air, he made her laugh, made her feel better about Willie being gone, and he gave her a book. Her very own book.

They heard a crash when Lise threw a pot at Jaden and stormed out the door. Everything became quiet, it was a relief for all of them.

Gunda, Jaden and Eddie had dinner together. The rest of the household was asleep. After dinner, Gunda decided that she was going to go to bed too. Molly asked for a glass of water, Gunda got up to go to the kitchen, but stopped at the doorway.

Jaden and Eddie were standing in the doorway. They were holding on to each other. She hoped that Jaden wasn't sick too. Gunda's eyes went wide with surprise when Eddie kissed Jaden on the cheek. She had never seen two men kiss before and didn't understand. She shrugged and went back into the bedroom. Molly would have to wait a little while for the water.

13

As the flu continue to grip Chicago everyone sheltered at home. The disease was so deadly that people were hiding in an effort to escape it. Only people who were considered essential were out in public.

There are five apartments in the building that the Michelsen's lived in. On the first floor the Bounce family lived. Chris, (Lise's lover or perhaps former lover) Elizabeth, and their sons, Elton and Brian. Across the hall from the Bounces were the buildings landlords and super, Mr. Richard Stanley, his wife Iris, and their 54-year-old son Paul.

Paul was always a strange one. Gunda frequently saw him walking up and down the staircases talking to himself. He would eat sandwiches placing crumbs down for the mice on every other step. He would sit on the landing and rock back and forth mumbling. Occasionally he would yell before starting to sing Christmas songs even if it was July and the temperature at 95. Sometimes Gunda sat and listened to him because he actually had a nice voice. Iris would come out of their apartment, climb the stairs and take him by the hand leading him back downstairs. Gunda thought he was the strangest person she had ever known. He was even weirder than Stanley Dotson who was in her grade at school. He Like to stick things up his nose. She figured Paul had to be crazy. He always walked in circles instead of a straight line.

The Millers lived on the second floor across the hall from the Prices. They had four children. Alan 6, Max 4, Patricia 10, and Jessica 11. The parents John and Judith both worked leaving 11-year-old Jessica in charge. Today the entire family was sick with the flu and no one was going anywhere. In two days they would all be dead except for four-year-old Max. He would become an orphan and a ward of the state.

The last family was the Price family. Father, Kenneth died in the accident two years ago. He had been hit by a car, his injuries were so severe he only lasted a few days.

What started as a minor accident became a fatal one for Kenneth. His car was hit from behind and when he got out inspecting the damage. He was standing behind the car when a third car hit the car behind his. Both his legs were severed when he was caught between the two cars. That left the mother, Martha as the sole support of her family. When Nicholas died last week it left Martha with only her daughter Anita.

Anita got up the next morning, feeling sick and went back to bed. Martha found her a few hours later, she had died from the flu. It could be that fast.

Martha was so distraught over the loss of her entire family that she took her own life. She sat down at the table and poured herself a glass of rat poison. When she finished she went laid down next to her dead daughter. Martha was found with a note in her left hand. She wanted her daughter and herself to be buried next to her son. She left the boy's information on the bottom of the note. What Martha didn't know was that Nicholas had been buried in one of those mass graves.

<p style="text-align:center">~~~</p>

The next morning was dark and dismal. Gunda watched as the rain turned to ice pellets beating against the window. It was early for the weather to turn from fall to winter, but it was known to snow in September. It was mid-October and the weather had turned very cold. Gunda thought it would probably snow tonight if it got any colder. The apartment was already turning cold and she would have to turn the oven on to keep it warmer. She would move everyone into the main room and close off the rest of the house in an effort to keep it warm. The crib wouldn't be a problem because it was on wheels. She, Michael, and Mable could sleep on a mattress, but she wasn't sure if she could manage to get it out of the bedroom without Molly's help and she was still sick. She thought that maybe Michael could help her, he was pretty strong for a five-year-old.

She looked over at her brother. He was playing with a wooden truck that Eddie had given to him. She went over and took him by the hand and explained what they had to do. It took her and Michael almost an hour to tug, drag, and push the mattress from the bed into the kitchen. Since space was limited she put Mable in with James. She would share the bed mattress with Molly and Michael. She hoped she wouldn't catch anything from Molly.

~~~

When Jaden came home the first thing he noticed was that the furniture had been rearranged. He wondered how Gunda got the mattress into the kitchen/dining area. He wasn't going to wake her to ask her, it could wait till tomorrow.

Jaden was as usual very tired. There was an old easy chair that sat off of the kitchen in the dining area. He decided that this would be where he'd sleep tonight because that way he could be close to the children.

Gunda woke up first, she grabbed her old, ratty bathrobe and pulled it around her. It was cold in the apartment. She stopped at the window when she noticed ice on the inside of it. She reached over and lightly put her hand on it. It was so cold that it felt hot. She went over and started the oven opening the door so that the hot air would come out into the room. She looked over at her father, his eyes were open so she went over to talk to him.

Gunda slowly let out the deep breath that she didn't even know she was holding. She whispered, "Father, I saw you kiss Eddie."
~~~

"You did?"

"Yes. Why did you do that?"

"He's my friend. A very good friend."

Being eight years old Gunda didn't say anymore. "Okay. I like him. He helps me."

Jaden took Gunda's hand in his and rubbed it. "I wish I could be here more, but I have to go to work every day."

"I know, but it's hard with Molly being so sick."

Jaden lightly touched her cheek and pulled her onto his lap. "I know. You're doing a great job. Michael is much better and so is Mable."

"Molly and James aren't any better. Can we get a Doctor for them?"

"There is no one. The entire city seems to be sick right now."

Gunda felt hot fear run through her. She had just realized that maybe Jaden could get sick. "Don't get sick Father."

"I won't. Eddie will be back to help you tomorrow. You need to rest as much as you can Gunda, I know this is hard for you."

~~~

When Gunda opened the door the next morning, Eddie smiled at her and handed her another book. She looked at it carefully turning it over in her hands. She loved the yellow cover. He told her it was a story about a little girl named Betsy who saved her dog. She held it tightly against her chest.

"Thank you Eddie. I never had such a wonderful present and now I have two books.

"Where is everyone?"
~~~

"Lise never came home last night. Molly and James are sleeping and Mable and Michael are playing together."

"We'll make breakfast for everybody in a minute, but first let's sit at the table. Bring your book."

Once they were seated at the table he pulled out a pencil from his pocket. "Let's write your name in the book so anyone who sees it knows that it belongs to you."

Gunda slowly shook her head. She knew that her printing was terrible. "You do it. If I write it nobody of be able to read it."

Eddie thought for a minute, winked at her and wrote:

To: my Gunda. Your second book from: your Eddie.

Gunda looked at what Eddie had written. She grinned at him, "Are you my Eddie?"

"Absolutely." He picked her up and hugged her before twirling her around the room. It made her laugh something she hadn't done in a very long time.

She giggled. "You're the best person I know."

Eddie helped Gunda with James and Molly. He is very concerned about Molly who seemed to be in and out of delirium. Gunda had moved everyone into the main room and had the oven going, but the apartment was still cold.

Gunda sat next to Molly on the mattress and looked up at Eddie, "she's so sick. Isn't there anything we can do for her? I gave her aspirin but it didn't seem to help."

Eddie leaned down and lightly put his hand on Molly's forehead, she was burning with fever. He knew that there was nothing they could do to help her. He placed a cool cloth on her head.

The door banged open and Lise stepped in. She had just come home from the hated job; it was one of the few places that was still open and working.

Eddie told her that he thought Molly had gotten worse. Lise gave him a nasty look and said, "You keep hanging around here, so you take care of her. I got that lousy job to go to."

"Lise," Eddie said quietly. "She's your daughter. The children need you right now."

"Yeah, well, I need something other than these brats. Get out of my way."

Lise pushed pass him and headed for her bedroom. "Why is it so cold in her?"

Gunda was sitting next to Molly and felt her take a deep breath before she quietly drifted away. She had been holding her hand when it went limp in hers. Molly had died. Tears rolled down her cheek as she tried to wish Molly alive.

She screamed. "Eddie, come quick."

Eddie felt for a pulse, but there was none. He placed his hand over her eyes and closed them.

Lise snorted at the news. She didn't shed one tear for her daughter. Truth be told she was actually glad that Molly was gone because it was one less mouth to feed.

Gunda ran to Eddie who held her tight. He took Gunda to the chair Jaden had occupied earlier and held her while she cried. He tried to console her as he rocked her in his arms.

"Why Eddie? Why?"

"Molly was very sick and couldn't fight anymore. I guess it was time for her to help God."

Gunda looked at Eddie with tear filled eyes. She buried her face in his chest and cried. "God already has Willie, why didn't he leave me Molly?"

"He must have needed her for something very special, something only she could do to help him."

"It's not fair. It's not fair."

Lise walked over and yanked Gunda away from Eddie screaming, "What are you doing here? Get out."

Eddie couldn't believe what Lise had just done. She was screaming at him and shaking Gunda while her daughter lay dead just a few feet away. He tried to keep his composure.

"Lise, I know you and I don't get along, but...."

"But nothing. Get out. Gunda, James is crying." She screamed and pushed her towards the crib.

"Lise, the child just lost her sister. What is wrong with you? Act like a mother."

Lise turned on Eddie. "You don't belong here. Leave my family alone, and stay away from my husband."

Lise didn't shed one tear over Molly's death. The truth was that she was glad that she was gone. It was one less mouth to feed. Gunda would have no time to grieve her sister because Lise wouldn't let her.

Gunda had taken James out of his crib and was holding him. She saw the anger in Lise and it was directed at Eddie. It wasn't fair because he had done nothing but help her. She wanted to go to him, but didn't want to cross Lise. She decided that she had to help Eddie like he had helped her. She placed James back into the crib. As she walked by Lise she was grabbed from behind and pushed against the wall. When Eddie moved forward to stop Lise, she slapped Gunda. Eddie moved fast and grabbed Lise's arm before she could strike the girl again.

"Enough!"

Gunda looked up at the window and heard the sleet pounding against it. It would soon turn to snow.

14

Lise stormed out of the apartment. Eddie gathered both Gunda and James into his arms. He held them until James stopped crying and hiccupped with the effort of it. He placed the baby back into his crib. Now that all was quiet James rolled over and immediately went to sleep. Michael and Mable were lying on a mattress near the kitchen, they both had ducked under the covers when Lise started yelling. Eddie walked over and peeked under the blanket.

"Come out, babies. Everything is going to be all right now."

When they didn't move he took Mable's little hand and drew her to him. Michael went to sit next to Gunda. She placed her arms around him protectively, the little boy shivered.

"It's okay, Michael, Lise is gone. I would never let her hurt you. You sit right here and I'm going to make something to eat."

While Gunda made the bottles for Mable and James, Eddie scrambled some eggs for himself, Gunda and Michael.

Michael ate his eggs with a ravished appetite, but Gunda pushed hers away. She looked up at Eddie and said, "I can't."

"I understand." Eddie said quietly. "Maybe later."

After Michael, Mable and James were sleep, Gunda asked Eddie to go with her to check on Molly. He took her hand and they went into the bedroom together.

"She looks just like she's sleeping." Gunda whispered. "Maybe she's going to be okay."

Eddie went down on one knee and looked into the little girl's eyes. "She's not sleeping, baby. Molly's in heaven with Willie now."

Gunda just stood there for several seconds before she leaned against Eddie. "I don't want her to go away."

"She has to go and take care of Willie."

Gunda took a step back. "We have to get father. He has to take Molly and put her next to Willie so they will have each other."

Eddie drew Gunda into his arms and held her tightly. Tears stung his eyes. He felt the little girl tremble and was helpless to help her deal with Molly's death.

"Your father should be home soon."

~~~

Lise ran down the steps to the first floor and over to Chris's apartment. She banged on the door until one of the twins answered. He knew immediately who she was. She looked at the boy and wondered which of them he was; she could never tell them apart and at this point could care less.

"Where's Chris?"

"My father is not here right now."

"Where the hell is he?"

"He and mother went to get some medicine for my brother. He's sick." The boy smiled slightly. "Would you like to come in and wait for him? He should be home very soon."

Lise barreled past the boy and charged into the house looking for Chris. When she got to his bedroom the boy stopped her from going in. "My brother. He's in there sick. You better not get too close to him."

She was satisfied that Chris wasn't there and went back to confront the boy.
~~~

"I'll wait. Are you sure that's where he went?" She asked as she plopped down in the chair.

The boy eyed her up and down but didn't answer her question. Instead he said, "Would you like something to drink? I could make tea."

"Okay, kid, but I'll have a whiskey and water."

The boy killer went over to the cabinet where his father kept the liquor and took out a bottle. Times had been hard and there was very little left, but he was going to give it to this woman. He grinned because he knew that this would be her last drink. He fingered the whiskey and looked at the clock over the stove. His father wouldn't be home for at least another two hours and his mother had actually gone to see his grandmother who lives alone and had become sick like so many others. He liked his grandmother and hoped that she would get well soon. His mother had been gone for two days and he didn't expect her home anytime soon. His brother wasn't actually home and probably wouldn't be any time soon. His brother liked to stay away. The boy killer suspected he was off drinking somewhere. At 15 his twin had taken a liking to alcohol and hung out with an older crowd of boys. He stayed away as much as possible.

It didn't matter to him because he had his own calling......he liked killing. His Father, he guessed was into whoring around and this bitch was probably one of his whores. His mother, well, she was weak and couldn't see anything that was going on right in front of her. He knew that she wouldn't see what he was about to do. If she standing right next to them in the room she still wouldn't see it.

~ ~ ~

When Lise didn't come home for four days, Jaden went to the 16th District Police Department for help. He was surprised to find only four officers in the entire building. There were a lot of people waiting in the lobby. He went up to the desk and talk to an officer who told him to sit down and wait his turn. Three hours later he finally had an interview with the Sgt. Gregory Everett.

"You have to understand Mr. Michelsen we have a skeletal staff at best. Like everyone else in the city they are all down with the flu."

"My wife is missing Sgt. Everett. She hasn't been home in four days and I've gone everywhere I can think of to look for her. I have children at home."

"We will do the best we can to find her. You need to tell me where you have gone to look for her so that we don't double check. I'll also need a description of her."

"I have a picture of her. It's old, but she hasn't changed much since this picture was taken."

Sgt. Everett mulled over the photograph. The picture was black and white and the woman it was wearing a hat that was pulled down over her eyes. The Sargent cleared his throat.

"What was she wearing last time you saw her?"

"Brown dress with a little white buttons down the front. Black shoes and an old gray hat with a feather on it. She had a flowered purse."

"What color are her eyes and what color hair does she have?"

"Brown hair and blue eyes."

"Does she have any scars or impairments?"

"No. No."

"Anything else you can tell me? Like why she would leave home?"

"I don't know why she would leave home. She's been having problems lately and has taken to drinking. I went by the bar that she hangs out at and they haven't seen her in days."

Jaden was dismissed with the promise that Sgt. Everett would notify him of any progress in finding his wife. He told him to go home and that she would probably turn up.

~~~

When Jaden arrived home Eddie was still there. He and the children were sitting down eating dinner. The house had been cleaned and each bed had been freshly made. For once in a long time the apartment smelled fresh and clean.

"Come and sit down Jaden."

Eddie placed a cup of coffee in front of Jaden. He sat down and stared into it. Eddie knew where he went and why. He turned to Gunda, "take the children into the bedroom so your father and I can talk."

She looked over at her father and slowly shook her head. "All right Eddie."

After the children left Eddie asked, "what happened?"

"The flu happened. It's all over the city and there are very few policemen over at the station house. They're all sick too. Sgt. Everett said if he finds out anything he'd contact me. Eddie, I don't think she'll ever come back. I have this deep down gut wrenching feeling that she won't. I'll never see her again. Things between Lise and me have been bad for a long time."

"Since you met me?"

"No, even before that. Eddie you and the kids are all that are keeping me going." Jaden looked deeply into Eddie's eyes and said, "I don't think I can make it without you. What we have probably
~~~

isn't fair to Lise because it's you I love, not her. I don't know if I ever really loved her and when she turned to drink I knew it was over. I wonder if that was my fault too?"

"No one forces you to drink Jaden. It's just a weakness and one that Lise can't overcome."

Jaden put his head into his hands and sighed deeply, "so much as happened in such a short time. Willie and Molly are both gone...... Dead. Now Lise has decided to disappear. I know she was with someone else, but she was still their mother. Not a good one. Not after the drinking started."

Eddie got up and put his hands on Jaden shoulders.

"Try not to think about it for right now. We can't change what's happening. Let's go to bed and things will look better tomorrow, who knows she might even show up."

"I have to report at 5 AM. You're right; I've never been so tired in my life. Let me make sure the kids are all in bed and kissed them good night."

Eddie held out his hand, "we'll do it together."

15

As much needed medical supplies grew shorter people continue to die. It was happening at alarming rate and Jaden's 12 hour day now became a 16 hour day.

Even medical personnel were dying as they were struck down by the flu. There were no beds in the hospital to put the sick in until one was vacated by someone who died of either the flu or pneumonia. The disease was taking a toll on the medical personnel. Many of the nurses were dying while taking care of flu victims. Mothers and fathers advertised in newspapers trying to place their children up for adoption. Every day big trucks would move caskets and transport them to the communicable graves. There was panic over the entire city and people were afraid to go in public even if they were wearing face masks. People were becoming so desperate that they would take clothing from the sick and pour oil on them right before setting them on fire.

~ ~ ~

Lise was getting tired of waiting for Chris. "Just when he is supposed to return because I'm not leaving here until we get a few things straightened out.

Elton placed a cup of tea on the table and slowly eased down on the chair across from her. "I'm sure father will be here soon. He said he wouldn't be gone that long."

Lise swept the teacup away from her splattering tea all over the threadbare carpet. She sneered at the boy across from her, "I don't want any more of your nasty tea."

Lise was furious, she felt the bastard was purposely avoiding her and she wouldn't have it. One way or another she was going to make him pay. She was pregnant with his damn baby and she wasn't going to take care of it alone, or support it alone. If necessary after she had the kid and if he didn't cooperate she would have no problem dumping it on his doorstep. Let his sweet little wife take care of his bastard child.

Lise was nervous, she got up and started to pace. "I can't wait around here all day. I thought you said he'd be home by now."

"He must've run into a problem. It's harder to get medicine now with everyone sick and maybe he had to go to several places."

"Look kid, take this crappy tea out of here and get me another whiskey."

Elton picked up the still half-full cup of tea from the floor and went to the kitchen. He placed the cup into the sink. There was a hallway behind the kitchen that led to the back of the apartment. To the left of that was a living room and to the right there were three bedrooms that branch off into another hallway.

Elton quietly opened his bedroom door just far enough to slip inside. He went to his bed and then down to his knees. From under the bed he pulled out a blanket which he carefully unfolded. Inside were six knives of various sizes. He lovingly picked them up and put them on the bed. He selected an 8 inch hunting knife and grinned.

Elton could be quiet when he had to, very quiet. He crept from the kitchen and back over to the family room. He looked in and grinned, Lise had her back to him. She was looking in her purse for something. He moved quickly over to the chair she was sitting in and raise the knife.

Lise had just looked into her compact mirror to check her lipstick when she saw Elton creeping up on her. She had time to rise up from her chair and drop the compact.

Elton raised his arm and brought it down in a swinging arc catching Lise's arm. She turned and with all her strength swung her purse hitting him in the face. The boy fell backwards striking his head on the floor. Lise bolted for the front door. She had it halfway open when Elton came up behind her and plunged the knife into her back. She screamed and turned on the boy striking out at him. He was much faster and sidestepped her leaving her failing her arms and trying to keep her balance. Elton grabbed her and spun her around so she was facing him when he plunged the knife into her heart. She didn't have time to even register the shock that she was dying. Ten seconds later she fell over dead.

Elton dispassionately watched as she slid to the ground. He looked at the room around him. There was a lot of blood and it seemed to be all over. He sneered down at the body and said, "Now look at the mess you made."

16

Elton whistled as he cleaned up the mess around him. He had taken the curtain from the bathroom and rolled Lise's body into it. She was heavier than he thought, but he managed to drag her over to the door and placed her next to it. He would take his father's car later and get rid of her. He washed down the floor and scrubbed the rug that had drops of blood on it. He took the bucket and went over to wash down the wall where blood had splattered on it. When he was done he stood back and looked at the room. He didn't see any blood anywhere and thought he had done a pretty good job.

Just as he was stripping out of his shirt his brother came in.

"What's that?" He asked pointing to Lise bundled up by the door.

"That's dad's girlfriend, his pregnant girlfriend."

Brian looked at him in shock. "What? Dad's got a girlfriend? She's pregnant?"

"Don't get excited Brian, I took care of the problem."

Brian sat down in the nearest chair. He was having trouble processing what his brother had just told him. He walked up and stood next to him as they both looked down at Lise's wrapped body.

"You...... You killed her?"

"Yeah, she was easy."

"Why? And....You can't leave a body in the house."

"She was trouble and now she isn't. Forget it Brian, she won't be a problem. I'm going to get her out of the here tonight." Elton turned so that he and his brother were face-to-face. "And you're going to help me."

Brain was horrified, he stuttered, "H...H... How?"

"We're going to take dad's car. We'll wait until after dark and then dump her in the trench where they are burying all of the flu victims. Nobody will notice another body."

"What if someone sees us?"

"No one will see us. We'll wait until they're at dinner."

Elton had stripped down to his short. He threw his bloody clothes to Brian. "Wrap these up with her while I get a shower and clean clothes."

~~~

The minute Elton came out of the shower his brother confronted him. "Elton, I don't know if I can do this."

"Yes you can. I'll take her legs."

When Brian didn't come to help him he dropped Lise's legs and stared at him. "I can't do this alone. She's too heavy. You stay here and I'll make sure the hallways clear and then we'll get her out of here."

Brian slowly walked over, looked down at Lise and sunk down onto the floor next to her. "All I want is for you to go away."

Elton casually walked down the hallway to the back of the building. He opened the back door that led into an alleyway and looked both ways. It was empty like most of the streets of Chicago had been for a long time. He slipped out and over to Leavitt Street where his father's car was parked. He pulled out the keys, got in and drove it over to the alleyway parking it close to the door. He looked around before he got out just to assure himself that he was alone. He went around to the front of the apartment and entered through the door, the hallway was empty. As he walked by the
~~~

stairway he looked underneath to make sure that Gunda wasn't hiding there.

It was 7 PM and the workers would've already gone to dinner. They would have to wait because he decided it would be safer to get rid of Lise after dark. He also knew that all of the workers would be gone by midnight. He wouldn't have known, but he had run into Jaden coming home from his burial detail late one night. He spoke to him for several minutes that night and discovered that the burial teams quit at midnight and started up again at 6 AM. It was a useful bit of information that he had stored away for later.

When Elton slipped back into the apartment he saw that Brian was still in the same place he had left him. He was leaning against the wall next to Lise.

"Everything's quiet. I put the car in the alleyway next to the back door so all we have to do is take her over to the car and dump her into the trunk."

"I can't." Brian said in a small voice. "I can't believe you killed her."

Elton leaned down to his brother and grabbed him by the front of his shirt. "You can and you will. I can't lift her alone. Now get a pair of balls and move your ass."

"But Elton...."

"Look Brian, there's no bringing her back, so the only choice is to get rid of the body."

Brian slowly shook his head. He knew that he had no choice but to help. Elton scared the hell out of him. He was deathly afraid of him and knew that he could and would kill him if he didn't help him.

Together they gathered up Lise's body and carried it down the hallway. Elton opened the door, they staggered under her heavy weight and over to the car. Somehow they managed to get her into the car's trunk.

"Get in."

"Elton......"

"Get in. I'll need help at the burial site."

Reluctantly, Brian went around to the passenger side of the car and got in. The two brothers didn't talk all the way to the site. The ride didn't take long. When they got to the burial site Elton pulled the car under a dark area next to a building.

"You wait here while I go and look around. Just relax Brian, nothing's going to happen."

While Brian waited for Elton, his level of anxiety grew. He swore that he could almost hear Lise calling to him from the trunk. He slapped his hands over his ears. When Elton knocked on the window he jumped so high he almost hit his head on the top of the car. Elton opened the door and laughed.

"It's not funny. You about scared me to death."

"There's nobody here. Nobody accepted dead folk. Come on. Let's hurry."

Getting Lise out of the trunk and down to the burial area seemed harder than when they put her in. "How come she got heavier?"

"She didn't get heavier Brian. Just keep moving and stop talking."

They dumped Lise's body in an area where there were at least two dozen other people. "Help me move this body, we'll put Lise underneath it."

"You want me to touch him? He looks moldy."

"Just get over here and help me."

Brian went over and helped turn the body of Jacob Harrison over onto his side. He was amazed how flexible the man was because he thought people went stiff after they died. They placed Lise underneath Jacob and rolled him back on top of her.

"Great." Elton laughed. "Now were done. Let's go home, I'm hungry."

17

Gunda was staring out of the window at the deserted street below her. Eddie leaned over and whispered, "It will come to an end soon."

"I want to go and visit with Molly and Willie, make sure that their resting easy."

Eddie sat down and pulled Gunda onto his lap, he hugged her. "I promise you that once it's safe again you and I will go together."

"I miss them so much."

Eddie rocked Gunda, she leaned her head against his shoulder. "I know baby. I wish I could bring them back to you, but no one can do that."

"I think I'm going to draw some roses and take them with us. We can put them on the graves."

"I think Molly and Willie would like that."

"Eddie, I was with John Poll the day before he died, how come I didn't get the flu and die?"

"You probably have a natural resistance to it, so you won't get it."

"Molly and Willie didn't?"

"No they didn't. It happens that way sometimes."

"That doesn't seem fair."

"Not all things are fair in life, Gunda. People dying is a fact of life." After a few minutes Eddie smiled at her. "Can you help me make dinner?"

Gunda jumped down from his lap and shook her head, "sure."

After dinner Michael wandered out of bed into the kitchen. Gunda looked at him, shook her head and took his hand. For some reason he was more restless and very cranky. She knew that it would take her a while to get him calm enough to lie down. She glanced up at the clock it was almost 11 PM. Father wouldn't be home for at least another hour and a half. Eddie had left earlier in the day saying that he had some business to take care and would probably not be back until tomorrow. Gunda looked around the quiet apartment, she missed Eddie.

Jaden came home late and went directly to bed, but the next morning he pulled Gunda aside to explain to her about her mother. He told her that her mother had disappeared and that she was presumed missing. Gunda had listened intently and now she had a question.

"What exactly does missing mean?"

Jaden leaned back in his chair and let out a deep breath. "No one knows where she is. She didn't go to her job and she hasn't come home."

"Did you look at the Tavern? She goes there a lot."

"How do you know that?"

"I followed her."

Jaden ate a simple meal of soup and bread before going back to his job. He said he probably wouldn't be home until late and she should take care of things.

The day went by quickly and when Gunda finally put the children to bed she was grateful they went quickly to sleep because she was tired. She wondered what happened to Eddie because he hadn't come back. She looked out the window in the darkness. She didn't know what she was about to witness. This was the night that Elton and Brian were getting rid of Lises' body.

It was cold again so she decided to make some soup. Gunda went over to the stove and put on the pot with the soup; she stirred it and waited for it to get hot. It smelled good and she didn't realize that she was hungry until she had started the soup. She took a bowl, filled it and took it to the table. As she lifted the spoon to her mouth she heard a noise coming from the hallway. She struggled and started to eat again. There was another noise that sounded like a thump.

Gunda went to the door and placed her ear to it. She heard nothing. Carefully, so she wouldn't make any noise she opened the door and looked out. She got down on her hands and knees and scooted over to the banister. She looked down to the hall below, the banister had pickets every 6 inches so she could see through them clearly. She was lying flat on her belly and saw 2 boys come into her sight line. They were carrying something heavy, but she couldn't figure out what it was. She knew it had to be heavy because they were struggling with it. The makeshift bag slipped between the first boy's hands and thumped to the ground.

Gunda squeezed her eyes tight trying to see who was carrying the bag, but it was so dark in the hallway she wasn't sure. It wasn't until they opened the back door and a light from the streetlamp outside flooded the door area that she saw Elton. At that very moment Elton looked up and spotted someone above them watching.

Gunda gasped and scurried backwards into the shadows. She was so scared she held her breath. She slapped her hand over her mouth so she wouldn't make any noise as her body started to shiver. She couldn't control the shaking and in her mind she saw Elton running up the stairs to confront her. After a few minutes when that didn't happen she carefully crept back over to the rail. She was just in time to see the door closing behind Elton.

Once the door closed behind them Gunda bolted for the apartment. She slammed the door shut and threw the bolt locking it. Slowly, she backed away from the door until she was sitting in Jaden's chair. "What was Elton carrying?" She whispered to herself. "That had to be his brother Brian with him."

Gunda walked back to the door and put her hands on it. She turned around, leaned against it and slowly settled down to the floor. Even at her young age she knew that what they carried in the shower curtain was a body. She could tell by the outline. She didn't know what to do. Her mother was missing and her father worked so much he was never around. She hoped Eddie would be back again tomorrow, but she couldn't tell him what she saw because she was afraid he would leave and not come back.

The next morning Gunda left the apartment early. Jaden had left even earlier and Eddie hadn't come back. Everyone was still asleep as she slipped out the door. She stopped and listened, the entire apartment building was quiet. She knew that the Stanley's were hiding inside their apartment too afraid to come out. She hadn't seen crazy Paul on the stairways in weeks. When Jaden sent her to pay the rent, Iris told her to slip it under the door. She was too afraid to even open it.

When she passed the Anderson apartment she stopped briefly. The Anderson's were new. They moved in after the Millers left and within two months, they were all dead. She stopped and stood in front of the Anderson's apartment door.

"I'm sorry."

~~~
~~~

The entire Anderson family had succumbed to the flu. The children were the first to die; four-year-old John couldn't fight the pneumonia that raged in his body. He went first. His 11-year-old sister, Christina died next. A week later 6-year-old Alvin and his 10-year-old sister, Sharon died on the same day.

Only their father Kenneth, and their mother, June were left. June became so despondent that she eventually took her own life. She took her husband's revolver, walked out into the deserted street in front of the apartment and put the gun to her head. Kenneth heard the gun shot and ran down to find his wife bleeding from a head wound. He sat down in the street and held her for the three hours it took her to die. No one came, no one called for help and during that time not one car passed by. Kenneth picked up his wife and took her to the where all the victims of the flu were being buried. Three days later he died from the flu.

18

The snow that had been threatening for weeks was finally falling. Gunda looked out the window at the soft covering, it made her feel good. She wrapped her coat tighter and slipped out the door. She went over to Francisco Street, crossed over to Bartow Avenue and down to the 16th precinct police department. The streets were still deserted and she didn't see a car or meet one person on the way. The only thing that was accompanying her was the cold wind that was blown in from the north. Somehow that always seemed to be a constant.

She walked into the station and was surprised that there was no one there. There were no policemen or even a clerk. She looked around the deserted station and called out, but no one answered her. Gunda walked around the Sargent's desk and opened the door behind it. There was a large room with many lockers and beyond that was a room with tables and chairs. She walked through both rooms and then went to another door, opened it and called out. She was met with silence. She looked around the room; it had racks and racks of rifles in it. There was a bookcase in the corner that had boxes of ammunition stacked into it.

Gunda turned around and followed the same path until she was back in the main room. She wondered where all the police had gone. The idea that the flu had affected the entire police force had never entered her mind. The few officers that had been left were out patrolling the streets, but they were stretched so thin that this was ineffective. Even though the flu ran rampant and everyone sheltered in their homes, the criminals were taking advantage of the situation. Crime had increased and many of the homes of the dead had been robbed. There was no one there to stop them. These thieves were all willing to take the chance of contacting the flu. Even the bodies that were in coffins waiting to be buried were searched for rings, earrings, and anything that would be worth money was taken from them.

Gunda looked around one more time and called out, but there was no one there to answer her.

~~~

She had gone to the police department with intentions of telling them what she saw. She didn't know what else to do so she went home, walking alone through the deserted streets of Chicago. She was actually happy that there was no one on the streets because she no longer wanted to talk to anyone.

~~~

Eddie arrived early at Jaden's apartment the next day and found that James was dead. Gunda had gently placed the sheet over him like she had done with Molly and Willie. The 10 month-old looked so small under the sheet. She told Eddie that James couldn't stop coughing.

"He started to breathe badly, like really, really fast and I didn't know what to do so I put a cold towel over him. He didn't get any better. When he turned blue I knew. Her voice got very low when she whispered, "And then he was just gone. He just stopped breathing."

Eddie took Gunda's hand and again led her over to Jaden's chair. He pulled her into his arms and held her.

Tears fell from Eddie's eyes. "I'm so sorry baby. I'm sorry I wasn't here to help you and be with you."

"Don't cry Eddie. I guess James just had to go and help with Mollie and Willie."

Eddie and Gunda cry together over the death of a helpless little boy who drifted away from them on a dark snowy day.

"Will we all die Eddie? It seems like everybody is dying."

"Don't think that way. We're going to be all right."

"Now, it's just father, you, me, Mabel, and Michael."

"Everything will work out."

Gunda placed James's blue blanket over him and patted his back. She wanted to do something more, but didn't know what. "I had to wrap James in his blanket. He always loved that blanket. When father comes home will he take James and put him with Mollie and Willie so they can be together?"

"Of course he will."

"When can we go visit them?"

"After everyone is over being sick. Then it will be safe to visit with them."

Mabel waddled out of her makeshift bed and went over to Gunda. She laid her head on Gunda's leg and patted her.

"Are you hungry Mabel?"

"Yes."

Gunda was suffering greatly by all the losses around her, but the little two-year-old needed her. She needed to be fed, so she put her sorrow away from her and took Mabel's hand and led her to the table. Gunda was actually confused by all that happened in such a short time. Her family was being taken and destroyed right before her. As much as she didn't want to be she was afraid. She was losing everything and then there was Elton. She shivered at the thought of him. She was almost sure that he knew it was her that night on the stairwell. Now, two days later she wasn't sure what she saw. She knew that they were carrying something, but what? It was all confusing in her mind.

All this was running through her mind as she made Mabel something to eat. Eddie, who had just come in, went over to the stove and took the eggs from her.

"I'll make breakfast. Scrambled eggs ladies?"

"Yeah." Mabel said jumping up and down.

"I don't think I can eat right now."

Eddie placed a kiss on Gunda's cheek. He smiled and said, "Maybe later."

When Jaden came home Eddie was the one to tell him about James death. The two men comforted each other and then Jaden wrapped James in a sheet and left the apartment with him. Gunda stood in front of the closed door. She put her head on it whispered, "Goodbye James. I love you."

Eddie couldn't help it, he enveloped Gunda into his arms and picked her up. He took her and sat down. Mabel and Michael ran over to join them. He gathered all of them into the chair and held them throughout the long day until the sun set.

He looked down at Gunda's makeshift bedroom in the kitchen. The landlord wouldn't give them any more heat and the apartment was actually cold. Many apartments still had fireplaces and there was one in the small living room in this one. He decided he would clean the fireplace and use it. He could put all the children in this room and keep them warm. It took him two days get the fireplace working and another day to move the three beds into the room. He also put a bed in there for himself. It was small and crowded, but with only the beds in it, it worked.

Eddie sat in Jaden's chair and thought about his home. He suggested to Jaden that he bring the children and move into his house which not only had several bedrooms, but better heat. Jaden wanted to stay hoping Lise would return. Eddie didn't understand why he cared for her because she had made it very clear that she couldn't care less about him or the children. He didn't agree with Jaden's decision, but he didn't want to push him right now. He was under a lot of stress working almost 16 hours a day and dealing with the deaths of all the flu victims. Even the long hours that all the workers were putting in couldn't keep up with the dead.

Jaden always came home exhausted and now he was dealing with the death of three of his children. He shook his head; all he could do was offer support and care for the other children.

19

Two weeks had gone by and Eddie became a constant in the Michelsen home. He made sure that there was always wood for the fireplace and cooked three meals a day. He read to the children before bedtime. He would go home from time to time but always returned the same day until one Monday. Eddie had left Sunday night and said he would be back soon. He didn't come home Sunday night, or the next night. Gunda was really worried that another person in her life had disappeared. She took her brother and sister into the living room and put them to bed. As she left the room she looked over at Eddie's empty bed.

"Eddie." She whispered. "Where are you?"

Gunda settled down with the book Eddie had given her. She was still sleeping in Jaden's chair when Eddie let himself into the apartment. He looked over at her and realized how young she was, too young to have all the responsibility that had been heaped on her. The chair with the three blankets engulfed her little body into a hug.

"Gunda." he said softly and shook her arm.

Gunda woke up slowly. She looked into Eddie's face and jumped into his arms. "I've missed you. Where did you go?"

"Let's make dinner."

"Dinner has been gone a long time ago."

"I'm hungry. Let's call it a late snack."

When the eggs were done, Eddie smiled and pointed to the table. "Come sit."

Mabel came over and tapped Eddie's leg. Tears ran down her face. He unconsciously picked up the little girl placing her on his lap and wiping away her tears. He leaned down and placed a kiss on top of her head. She looked up at him, patted his cheek and giggled. He kissed her nose and handed her the spoon which she happily chewed on.

"I didn't want to stay away, but there was no choice. My mother. She was ill."

Gunda's eyes got wide, "she got the flu?"

"Yes. She was old and it was very hard for her to fight it. I had to take care of things."

Gunda walked over and put her arms around Eddie's leaning against him. In a small voice she said, "I'm so sorry Eddie."

Eddie pulled her into his arms next to Mabel. He was overwhelmed with emotion and started to cry as he rocked both the children.

"When will it ever end?"

~~~

While the flu ran rampant in Chicago killing everyone in its path, another type the killer was also searching for his next victim. Elton was almost certain that the kid on the third floor saw them the night he and Brian carried Lise out of the building. He knew it had to be that Gunda kid. He also knew they had to protect his dirty little secrets and that meant he would have to get rid of her. He went to search for his brother.

"Brian, I need your help."

Brian looked up from the book he was reading. He was deathly afraid of his brother and uncomfortable even being in the same room with him. He looked around for his mother.
~~~

"Forget it. She's out." Elton laughed. "Don't be a friary cat." He was sitting on the back of the chair and jumped down from it. "Dear old mother has a boyfriend. Fred something. She's with him today, so it's just you and me brother. He went over and stood in front of Brian. "You're going to help me or I will make you regret it. Understand?" Elton reached into his pocket and pulled out a knife. He held it under Brian's chin and sneered. "You're always going to help me. We're brothers. And brothers help each other."

Brian slowly shook his head. "Okay." He said as he leaned back as far as he could in the chair.

Elton began to pace back and forth and then stopped in front of his brother. "That kid upstairs, that Gunda, she saw us. I just know she did."

"What are you going to do?"

"Wait till she's alone and then you and I are going to take care of this problem."

Brian definitely knew what take care of the problem meant, Lise had been the problem, and now she was dead."

20

Gunda stared out the window at the new blanketing of snow. It'd been so long since she left the apartment, she felt like she was in prison.

Michael and Molly were sleeping and Eddie had gone for groceries. Before he left he asked if she would be all right until he came back.

"It's all right. I can take care of Mabel and Michael. I've done it before."

"I may be gone for quite a while. All the stores around here have closed so I have to go the other side of the city."

Gunda had gotten a little nervous at that and asked tentatively, "how long?"

"I'll try to make it fast. I'm going to get enough food to last us for a long while so I won't have to leave so often. Come on over here and give me a hug for my journey."

She threw her arms around Eddie and squeezed tightly. "Come back soon."

Gunda sat down at the table and gazed into her soup. She sighed. "Lise where are you?"

She took the soup over to Jaden's chair and eased back into its comfort. She thought about Lise and wondered for the hundredth time where she was and why she didn't come back, not that she had spent much time here. Her thoughts went back to the night in the hallway. She checked the calendar this morning and realized it'd been 21 days since Lise did her disappearing act. Twenty one days since the hall. Lise had never been gone this long. The last time she had been gone it was for three days. Jaden found her drunk at the Tavern. No surprise there. Gunda didn't mind that she was gone because all she did was scream at Jaden, or one of them. She was the noisiest person that she ever knew. What she really didn't understand was how she could be so cold and uncaring about her own children. Gunda didn't believe that she would ever return. Visions of the hall came back to her. *Could the bundle in the hall been Lise?*

Gunda leaned back and closed her eyes, she realized how very quiet it was, no noise. The silence was deafening but welcomed. Somehow the absence of sound suited her troubled mind. She felt the silence from the tip of her head all the way to the bottom of her toes and it warmed her. It brought her a comfort she hadn't had in a very long time. In a strange way she felt better. She hoped that it would last. Her good feelings didn't last for long.

There was a loud banging on the door. She stared at the door as fear leaped into her, from the other room Mabel started crying when she was awakened from the banging. Gunda ignored her and cautiously walked over to the door, the banging continued. She looked over at the kitchen sink and saw a large knife which she took and held in front of her. She briefly wondered if she could use it on whatever was knocking on the front door so furiously. She raised her arm as she slowly went forward toward the door. She felt like she was walking through a thick fog that tried to keep pulling her back. She realized that she was afraid. More scared than she had ever been her life. More scared than when Molly, Willie and James had died.

Gunda put her hand on the doorknob and slowly turned. With a deep breath she flung open the door, hand held high ready to strike. The knife dropped out of her hand with a loud thud. There was no one there.

21

Elton was under the stairs laughing. He covered his mouth with his hand to keep from being heard. He was going to kill the little bitch tonight, but she had kept her mouth shut about what she saw so he decided maybe have some fun with her before he killed her. He would have to get her alone. It seemed like there was always someone around. He also knew that he would have to be very careful. Elton scooted out of his hiding spot and went back to his apartment.

"Where have you been?" Brian asked.

"None your business. Go play with your little boy toys."

"You were up there. You were pounding on her door. I heard you. Leave her alone, Elton, I don't think she knows anything."

Elton was fast; he grabbed Brian by the shirt and backed him up against the wall. "Listen up brother. No one can know what we did. We! You're in this as deep as I am, and your ass is on the line as well as mine so keep your mouth shut!

"Elton......"

Elton slammed his brother up against the wall again. "Shut up. I have to think."

"What's going on boys?"

Elton turned to his father and gave him his best smile. "Father. We were wondering when you would come home."

"I'll be home until his flu thing is over. The plant closed."

Elton lay on his bed staring at the ceiling. He was beyond furious. With his father home he would be limited to what he could do. He had to get rid of Gunda and this would make it even harder, and then there was his brother. He had a big mouth and couldn't be trusted. He never should have involved him and now he feared he would have to kill both of them and then melt into the orphan system. He would just bet that he could get lost in it easily; all he had to do is change his name. It would actually give him more freedom. His friend, Randall Barkley had been in the orphan's home for some time now. They went to school together for years and Randall was considered an orphan because he was under 18 and had no parents.

Randall was 14 in 1917 and too old for adoption, he was transitioned into the hands of stern caretakers at the orphanage where all he found was constant hunger. No adoption for him. One day they came for Randall and told him to follow them which he did. He was scrubbed, given new clothes and put onto a west bound train. He became what thousands of children were, a part of a migration. He was sent to New York and became part of what was known as the orphan train. All the children on the train acquired new homes. The children would be put on display for farmers in need of help, but some of them would become nothing more than slaves. Family members would go to the train and choose children to help with their sick, or to work from sun up to sun down on farms. Some of the children were lucky to get parents who truly wanted them and would give them a good life, but some suffered abuse and were treated worse than hired help.

Elton decided that after he killed his father and brother he would be free for the first time, truly free. He supposed he would have to include his mother or she would become a problem to him. He hoped that she would run off with her new boyfriend and save him the trouble of getting rid of her, but that didn't look like it was going to happen. He wasn't really worried about the orphanage because he didn't plan on staying there long. He could take care of himself and he was very comfortable living on the streets. He made friends in the streets and disappeared for days at a time with them. He went with the gang of boys and hung out with them, learned from them. They knew how to steal for a living, something they taught him. He was very good at it. This damn flu had put a stop to a lot of his theft, but it wouldn't last forever, and he still had a lot of money hidden away. Now all he had a do was wait for the right time. His nosey brother wouldn't be a problem, but father had to go first because he might be a problem. He was bigger and stronger than him. If he wasn't careful he could overpower him. It was too bad that he had lost his job because that had sealed his fate.

~~~

Within the next two weeks the flu took a turn for the worst and even more people were becoming victims of it. Elton smiled when he read the headlines because it was perfect. He could kill his father and deposit him with the rest of the flu victims. No one had found Lise and it was assumed that she had run away to a new life. If he was lucky he could keep it quiet that his father, mother, and brother were gone. He intended to have Brian help him with their father, but then he had to go too. If things worked out right maybe he could kill both of them at the burial site. He would tell father that Jaden had secured a job for him. He looked at the headlines again.

THE HEADLINE READ:

STAY ALIVE...STAY INSIDE
~~~

22

After Jaden got off of work, and put in a 16 hour day, he once again tried to find Lise. He had a good idea where to start. He sat down in an empty doorway and re-read the paper he found at the bottom of the dresser drawer in their bedroom. It was to Chris Bounce, the man who lived downstairs from him.

Dear Chris,

First let me confess that I love you and I always will, but don't let that make you think that I will ever back down. I thought you felt the same way about me, but now I see that I am wrong.

I don't care that you are married or that I am married. You said we would be together forever and I believed you. YOU LIED........... I now believe that you lied to me all along.

The minute you found out I was pregnant with your baby, and this baby is yours, you tried to get rid of me. This baby is your responsibility and you will be responsible for it, or I will go to your precious wife and give her the facts. This kid is going to keep us together forever. I don't love Jaden, or want his ungrateful brats. All they do is whine. Meet me tomorrow at our place or you'll regret it.

Lise

Jaden re-read the letter for the fifth time. When he found it, it was crumbled and thrown into a ball at the bottom of the dresser. It appeared that she had written another letter and he wondered if it was the same thing. Was this a copy of what she sent?

He got up stretched and decided it was time to confront Chris and find out what happened to Lise, but first he was going to go to 'their place'. He knew where that place was, a tavern not far from where they lived.

Jaden found the tavern closed. There was a light coming from in the back somewhere so he banged on the door. He waited a few minutes and banged again. Someone from inside yelled, "who is it? We're closed. The flu thing."

"Are you the owner? I need to talk to you."

"Go away."

"Please, I need to talk to you. I'll only be a minute. I'm looking for my wife."

"Okay. Okay. Hold on a minute."

Bill Blackman, the owner of the tavern walked back to the bar and placed the revolver he had in his hand underneath it. It was a few minutes before Jaden heard the click of the door lock. An older tall man stood in front of him, his gray hair was long and he looked very tired.

"Come on in."

The tavern was dark, but the man flipped on the light as he headed towards the bar. "I'm Bill Blackman."

"Jaden Michelsen. I live just down the block and I'm looking for my wife, her name is Lise."

Jaden pulled out his wallet and produced a picture of her. Bill placed a beer in front of him and took the picture.

"Beer's on the house. Let me just give a good look at this picture."

Bill studied the picture for a good five minutes before he handed it back to Jaden. "I know her." He said as he drew another beer and put it down on the bar front of him.

"I know her." He said and took a drink of his beer. "She came in here every Tuesday and Thursday. There was a man with her and they drank hard, but always paid the bill and didn't to disturb anyone."

My wife hasn't been seen in a couple of weeks. I went to the police, but with what's going on I couldn't get much help."

"Yeah. Hard times for everyone. I may lose this place if I can't open up soon, it's probably dead already."

Jaden looked carefully at Bill for the first time. He was around 55 years old and had probably worked hard all his life to make this tavern a go. If he lost his business he wondered what he would do.

"Sorry."

"Not your fault. The way of things. Last time I saw your wife was about three weeks ago probably right before I closed my doors. She was with that man. All I know about him is his name, she called him, Chris."

Jaden finished his beer and held out his hand. "Thank you for your help and the beer."

"My best to you. I hope you find her."

~ ~ ~

After Jaden left, Bill Blackman, locked the door and turned off the lights. He went to the safe and took out all of the money he had left in the world. It totaled $109.86. He put the money on the bar top with a note that said one word.............sorry.

Bill went back and retrieved the revolver from under the bar. He went to a back room where he had a cot that he sometimes slept on if it got late he didn't want to go home. He took off his shoes, lay down on the cot and covered himself with a blanket. After a few minutes he took a deep breath and pulled the trigger.

~ ~ ~

Jaden hurried home, but before he went to his apartment he went over to Chris Bounces. He pounded on the door. There was no answer so he went to the foyer and found the bell for the Bounce apartment and pushed it before going back to pound on the door again. No one answered.

Jaden wondered why they weren't home. No one was supposed to be out on the streets and everyone he knew had sheltered into place. He decided if they were in there no one was going to answer. He slowly walked away and took the stairs up to his own apartment. There would be another time.

23

Jaden threw the Chicago Tribune onto the kitchen table. The house was very quiet. He looked into the fireplace room and found the sleeping children. They were still bunking in there because it was warmer. Eddie was also sleep. He went to his bedroom, piled several blankets on the bed, crawled under them and was instantly asleep. He was exhausted. He didn't even bother to remove his clothing.

When Gunda got up the next morning, she didn't see Jaden and thought he was already gone for the day. Eddie and the other children were still asleep. She took a blanket and wrapped herself in it, then went to the sink and got a glass of water before sitting at the table. The first thing she noticed was the paper. She opened it and spread it out on the table.

On the front page was a picture of several Red Cross Motor Corps (nurses) on duty. They held stretchers in front of an ambulance. Everyone had their faces covered with masks. The article said that at this point one third of the world was sick with the flu. "I wonder how big a third of the world is?"

The paper also stated that there was no test for it, or a cure. Doctors could only provide supportive care to the victims. She studied the second picture in the article; it had roles of cots with victims of the flu. It was the soldiers from Fort Riley in Kansas.

The paper also provided a list of things on how to protect yourself. On the list they advised:

Cough and sneeze into a handkerchief.

If you are working, you should walk there.

No spitting on sidewalks.

Don't use common towels with anyone.

Get a lot of rest.

Avoid crowds and stay inside.

If sick seek a Doctor. This applied to fever, colds, pneumonia, and bronchitis.

Gunda re-read the list for the third time. "Avoid crowds?" She looked out at the snowy day. The streets as usual were deserted. "It's real easy to avoid crowds, there aren't any?"

She turned the page and continued to read. This page offered 'remedies' to cure the flu. She shook her head and thought that if these remedies would work then no one would be sick.

She turned the page again and continued to read about the flu. She skipped the words she didn't understand. Actually, she didn't understand any of it. She tired of the paper after she read about the no smoking band, she folded the paper and pushed it away from her.

"Good morning."

"Hi Eddie, I didn't want to wake you. I was reading the paper."

"Anything good in it?"

"No, just more dead people. Is this flu thing ever going to end? I'm tired of being cooped up in the house."

Eddie made himself a cup of coffee and sat down. He picked up the front page of paper.

It read:

FLU CONTINUES WITH MORE DEATHS

"It will Gunda, but I'm afraid it will take a long time."

"It seems like the whole city is dead. Last time I went to the grocery store I didn't see one person and there were only two people there at the store.

"People are afraid and staying at home."

Jaden came out of the bedroom and yawned.

"Jaden, we didn't know you were home. Do you want a cup of coffee?"

"I needed some sleep. This working 16 hours a day is starting to get to me. I was very tired."

Eddie handed Jaden's his coffee cup and went to get another one. He took a sip and looked at the cup. "Coffee? Since when do we have coffee in this house?"

"I brought it. You can't start a day without a decent cup of coffee. It just as in civilized."

Jaden deposited himself into a chair. "The world's not a very civilized place today. If people keep dying we won't have to worry about it."

"Father, where are Molly, Willie, and James buried? I want to take them some flowers."

"It's winter Gunda. There are no flowers right now. Come spring when this flu is gone we'll all go and bring flowers. Right now it's just too dangerous."

"How can be dangerous?"

Eddie took a sip of his coffee and looked over the cup at her. "Too many sick people baby."

"We're just going to see someone who's dead."

"It's still too dangerous."

"Father, have you found Lis........ Mother?"

"No, but they're still looking. I haven't heard anything yet."

~~~

An hour later Jaden left for work, but before he left the building he stopped at Chris's apartment. He answered the door this time and Jaden pushed his way in.

"I'm looking for my wife."

"I don't have her. Who's your wife?"

"Don't play dumb. I know that you've been seeing her."

Jaden held out the letter he had found. "Read it."

Chris quickly read the letter and decided it had to be a copy. The bitch left him a copy indicating he was the father of her unborn child.

"This is crazy. I only know your wife from the plant. We both worked there on the assembly line, but I never had a relationship with her. Ask her. Bring her down here and ask her."

"I can't bring her here. She's missing."

Chris changed his demeanor and got an appropriate amount of sadness in his voice. "I'm so sorry. I don't know where your wife is and I never had an affair with her. We're just friendly, that's all."

Jaden didn't know what to say. Was this a fantasy that she had? Was this an affair in her mind or was Chris lying through his teeth? He had no way of knowing. He took a deep breath and asked, "When was the last time you saw her?"

"At work. Come to think of it she hasn't been there quite a while. I'd say two weeks or better. That would be the last time."
~~~

While Jaden and Chris talked, Elton stood just out of sight listening. His bastard father was going to crack. He wasn't strong like he was. Even he could hear the lie in his voice. He had to do something and do it fast. Maybe he should just kill the fool.

"If you know where she is...."

"I don't. I'm not involved with your wife."

Chris threw the letter at Jaden "you need to leave."

~ ~ ~

Jaden was late for work, but he didn't care. As he walked on he decided he would have to give up on Lise. Even if he found her, she wouldn't come back. He wondered why he even cared. He had lost her a long time ago. She didn't love him, but he had thought she would stay because of the children.

When he got to the front of the graveyard he stopped and looked up at the fence. It was then, at that very moment, and in this spot that he realized Lise was truly gone to him. Somehow, he couldn't even get up the energy to care anymore.

"Goodbye Lise."

24

Gunda sat down at the kitchen table and touched the paper that Jaden had brought home. She flipped the folded paper open, closed her eyes and randomly pointed her finger at an article.

It read:

Chicago police officers ordered to arrest anyone who coughs or spits in public.

"Spitting is nasty." She said and continued to read the other reports in the paper.

As the killer virus continues, the city is being overtaxed and acute shortages of all medical care are being felt everywhere. There are Doctor Shortages, nurse shortages, and all auxiliary help in the medical field. Citizens are urged to continue home isolation.

As Gunda was folding the paper she felt a tap on her arm. Michael stood next to her with Mabel.

"We're hungry."

"Okay. Is Eddie still sleeping?"

Michael looked over at the fireplace room and shook his head. "He's tired."

"I'll make you breakfast."

~~~

Elton went over to where his brother was sitting and slugged him in the shoulder. "Brian, come with me."

Brian looked up from the book he was reading. Rubbing his arm he asked, "where?"

"We need to talk in private."
~~~

"Why?"

"Just move your ass. Now!"

Brian mumbled to himself as he slowly got up and followed his brother. "Okay."

Elton and Brian went downstairs to the basement area behind the furnace and sat down on the dirty concrete. A rat came over to investigate them and Elton kicked at it. The rat scurried away and disappeared into the darkness beyond the furnace.

"It's nasty down here. Filthy dirty. Why did we have to come here and what do you want?"

"I have something very important that needs to be done and I can't do it alone. You're going to have to help me."

Brian broke out in a sweat despite the cold. He tentatively asked, "What?"

"I need to eliminate someone. We need to eliminate someone."

"We?? Who? I don't want to kill anyone."

Elton pushed Brian against the wall. "We brother. It has to be done before he finds out about me and I don't want any crap from you. No discussion on this. We're going to kill father."

"Father? You want to kill our father? Are you crazy? The lady was bad enough. Horrible. I can't get her out of my mind. It disturbs my sleep, I can't sleep. I, I won't do it. I can't do it. How can you think about killing Father?"

"Shut up." Elton pushed him back against the wall and again pulled out his knife holding it against his throat. Brian's eyes went wide with fear. "I don't care about your nightmares or that you can't sleep. I need you to help me, there is no one else and if you don't you'll be the first to die. I don't want to kill you Brian."

~ ~ ~

Elton spent the next four days planning his father's death. He laughed to himself because he planned to dump him with his lover, Lise. He felt it was only fitting that they should be together in the end. They will be with the rest of the losers of this world.

He waited for just the perfect time, it came when Chris left the apartment early in the afternoon. Elton started a search for money. He would need money after everything was over. Briefly, he wondered where his mother was whoring around today. It really didn't matter because she usually showed up at five. He hoped she would stay away, run off with whomever so he wouldn't have to kill her.

"Less trouble that way."

If she did come back he would take care of it. After he killed both of them it would be off to the landfill for them. He loved to think of that mass burial site as the landfill. Useless throw away people were buried there.

Elton had snuck out three nights ago and watched the burials; he also discovered that they changed the schedule. He had been going for at least a month to observe when they took breaks and how long they were gone. When they took Lise there they had been lucky and he didn't encounter anyone, but he didn't want to take that chance again. Now, he discovered that they had changed their break time from midnight to two in the morning. It was a big inconvenience, but it was important information. If he had come at midnight with two bodies it could've been a disaster.

Elton decided to delay the murders of his parents and his brother for two weeks. He wanted to make sure that they would keep this new schedule. It wasn't a big thing, but inconvenient.

As he walked home he thought about Gunda. It was time to have a little fun with her because, after all, he needed something to do for fun while he waited. He planned on killing her on the same night and just add her to the body count.

He laughed. "That will save me a trip to the burial yard."

~~~

Gunda searched the apartment again. She couldn't find Michael. She looked down at the snowy city streets and wondered if he was outside. Eddie had left early this morning to go for groceries and wouldn't be back for at least another hour. She went and checked on Mabel who was still sound asleep in the fireplace room. She kicked off her blanket, so she pulled it up and covered her before leaving. Mabel would sleep for a while and wouldn't know that she was gone.

Gunda slipped on her coat and went down the stairs. She opened the door and stepped out into what was a very cold day. She called out, "Michael. Michael."

When she didn't get an answer she started to walk and went two blocks in each direction, but no Michael. The streets were deadly silent just like the rest of the city had become. She not only didn't see Michael, she saw no one else either. Her only company was the constant blowing of the wind which had become relentless. Since she didn't know what else to do she went back to the apartment to check on Mabel.

She stopped at the door and turned to look at the snowy streets, "Michael where are you?"

Gunda pushed the door open and entered the apartment building. She was cold, wet, and now hungry. When she felt the small difference in the temperature she sighed with relief. She hadn't realized how cold she was. It wasn't that it was that much
~~~

warmer inside, but just getting out of the wind helped. She brushed off the snow on her coat and went up the stairs.

Gunda pulled the key from around her neck and use it to get in the apartment. Everything was quiet. She peeked into the fireplace room where Mabel was still sleeping. She hadn't spotted the note that was on the floor. It had been shoved under the door. She walked over and picked it up.

She opened it and read:

'Michael's in the basement with the rats.'

Gunda dropped the note, pulled open the door and ran right into Eddie. He laughed as he grabbed her so she wouldn't fall. "Slow down."

"We need to save Michael. Hurry Eddie."

"What? Why does Michael need saving? Where is he?"

"In the basement. With the rats. We need to hurry."

Eddie didn't ask any more questions. He quickly placed the bags of groceries on the table and followed Gunda downstairs to the basement door.

Gunda pointed under the stairs. "The doors under here. Behind the wagon."

Eddie pulled out the wagon and flipped the lock on the door. He turned to Gunda and asked, "Why do you think he's down here?"

"The note."

"What note?"

"The one under the door. I'll show you later."

Eddie knelt down so he was at Gunda's level. "I want you to stay here. It's very dark down there and I don't want you to get hurt. If Michael's down there I'll find him."

"Eddie, I want to go with you."

Eddie pulled out a pack of matches and lit one holding it into the doorway. There were four stairs that led down to even darker hallway.

"You need to stay here. I'll go down and have a look."

"Please Eddie, let me go with you."

"You need to wait here."

"Hurry."

Eddie lit another match and continued down the long hallway that led to the furnace room. It was so dark that he needed to go very slow. He heard the squeak of the rats that Gunda had mentioned. He didn't like rodents of any kind and shivered. At one point he touched the wall and it felt wet. He quickly drew back his hand.

"Michael. Michael, are you down here?"

When he didn't hear an answer he continued down the corridor until finally he reached a 10 x 10 room. At the very top near the ceiling there were two small windows that let in some light. He should have brought a flashlight. He lit another match and held above his head trying to see what was in the room.

There was a large round object in the center of the room which had to be the furnace. In one corner there was a small bench filled with tools.

"Michael."

Eddie heard a cough and turned to the other side of the room. Lying in the corner was a small bundle. He strained his eyes trying to make out what it was when the bundle moved. Again he heard the squeak of rats. It gave him the chills.

Eddie called softly. "Michael?"

Muffled groans came from the bundle. Eddie quickly went over to Michael. He had a black bag over his head and his hands were tied behind his back. When Eddie touched him he yelled.

"It's all right Michael. It's me, Eddie. Are you all right?

Michael started to cough harder as Eddie tried to remove the bag from his head. Finally, after what seemed like forever he ripped a hole in it. The little boy gasped in great gulps of air.

Eddie struck another match that lit up the tear stained face of Michael. He held the match up to his face and then dropped it and pulled Michael into his arms.

"You're okay now, I'm going to get you out of here. Michael, I'm going to pick you up and carry you. I'll untie you when we get out of here and I can see what I'm doing. You're alright now. You're safe with me."

Eddie hurried through the hallway and up the four stairs.

"Michael." Gunda cried.

Michael who had been silent started to cry again. Eddie quickly untied the ropes and freed Michael's arms. He threw himself into Eddie and clung to him as he sobbed.

"Run up and open the door Gunda."

She raced up stairs and waited with the door open as Eddie carried Michael up. Once they were all in the apartment, Gunda closed the door behind them.

"Go get Michael a blanket."

"I'll be right back."

Gunda, bring the blanket into the fireplace room. It's warmer in there."

She got the blanket and followed closely behind Eddie. Earlier they had moved a chair into the room, Eddie sat down with Michael secured in his arms. Gunda put the blanket around both of them.

"Do you want me to make some soup? I think there's a little left."

"I'll get the soup. Be right back."

Eddie placed Gunda in the chair next to Michael. She put her arm around the little boy and he buried his face into her chest. Before he left Eddie wrapped the blanket around both of the children and kissed them.

"I'll be right back. You'll be all right baby." He said to Michael.

Michael shook his head, but didn't look at him. Eddie went downstairs to the hall phone and called for the police. The patrolman on duty promised that they would have someone come out and take a report.

After Eddie heated the remaining soup he took it in to Michael. Gunda put the bowl on her lap and started to spoon feed him.

"Eddie." Mabel said pointing to him.

"Did you have a good nap, sweetheart?"

She giggled. "Eddie."

Eddie went back to the kitchen and fixed Mabel a bottle of milk. She took it and lay down on her pillow.

"Michael said a big man took him."

"Is that right Michael? Do you know who this big man is?" Michael shook his head no.

Michael hesitated and then said, "He.......... He put the bag on my face and I couldn't see."

Eddie stroked Michael's cheek. "It's all right, Michael, you're safe now."

"There was a knock on the door. He.....he called through the door. Michael! Michael! Come out and play with me. I opened it and the big man pushed me down. He put the bag over my face and he hurt me. He hit me in the stomach and then tied my hands. I didn't know where I was and then you came and found me. I was so afraid. I could hear the strange noises."

Michael started to cry, Eddie picked him up, held him close. He continued to tell him that he was safe. Mabel looked up, dropped her bottle and searched for her bear. She waddled over to Michael and handed it to him.

He reached up and took it from her. "Thanks Mabel." He sniffed.

25

Patrolman Lionel Brakeman sat at the kitchen table writing his report.

"What time did you first discover him missing?"

"After I checked on Mabel." Gunda offered.

"You know what time that would be?"

Gunda looked over at Eddie and shrugged. "Not sure, but it was before you came home. You had already gone for the groceries."

"I left about 9 AM and came home around 11 AM. Gunda and I went to the basement and we found Michael."

"Here's the note that someone shoved under the door."

Patrolman Brakeman took the note from Gunda. "Do you know who wrote this?"

"No."

Michael walked into the kitchen still wrapped in a blanket. He went directly to Eddie who picked him up. Patrolman Brakeman looked at the small boy.

"Is this Michael?"

"Yes."

"Michael, do you know who did this to you?"

Michael buried his face and Eddie's shirt. "I don't think Michael knows anything. His face was covered by a bag."

"Do you have that bag?"

"I'll get it Eddie." Gunda said and ran over to the fireplace room. A few minutes later she came back with the black bag and handed it to the policeman.

Office Brakeman tuned the bag over in his hand as he examined it. "There seems to be nothing unusual about this bag. I'll file a report and when the investigator is available he will contact you."

"Do you have any idea when that would be?"

"With what's going on the city were very short staffed. We have only 10 patrolmen in the district that aren't sick with the flu. I'm afraid it will be awhile."

The police never came to investigate after that first day.

~~~

The next day Eddie called the children to him. They were in the fireplace room because the weather had turned even colder and it was the only room that was reasonably warm. He made sure that they were all wrapped in blankets before he started. Gunda and Michael sat together on the mattress they had thrown on the floor. Mabel lay next to them hugging her faded green bear.

"I want you to listen very carefully to me. There are times when I will have to leave here. Go to the store......"

Eddie." Michael interrupted. "Where's father?"

"He's working."

"He hasn't been home in days."

"These are very hard times Michael and many people need to be taken care of. What he's doing is very important for the entire city."

Gunda smiled. "I'm glad you're here with us Eddie."
~~~

"And I want to keep you safe. That's what we need to discuss right now. You are not to open the door for anyone but me. I don't want you to go outside alone. Michael that means I have to be with you. Someone took Michael and we don't know who and I don't think the police are going to be here any time soon to help us. I don't want this to happen again to anyone of my children."

"Why would someone try to take Michael?"

"I don't know Gunda, but we won't let hit happen again. Now, who's hungry?"

~~~

The weeks dragged on with no more incidents. Eddie made sure he was there as much as possible and warned the children when he left the house that they should stay in and not answer the door. Jaden came home only occasionally as the need for more burials grew. When he was there he slept, ate and went back to work. There was little said between him and the children, there never seemed to be enough time. Since Lise was still missing Eddie found that he had taken over her role in the home. He cared for the children, fed them, and made sure that he read them a short story before bedtime. He played with them and told them stories.

Actually, in many ways he was a better mother to them than Lise ever was. He even went down to talk to the landlord through the door because they wouldn't open it. He did manage to get a little more heat into the apartment.

Eddie's arrangement with Jaden and the children worked out well for all of them. He had asked Jaden if he found out any new information on Lise, but it was like she disappeared into the night. She would just become another missing person in the police department's cold case department.
~~~

26

Elton waited patiently for his father to come home. Chris was one of the many who did not adhere to any of the restrictions put on him by the city of Chicago. He didn't wear a mask or even bothered to wash his hands when he came home. He did what he wanted, when he wanted, and everyone else can be damned.

When Chris was leaving, Elton asked his father where he was going and received a crack in the mouth for his inquiry. It had been that way since he was a small child.

Elton was furious when Chris slammed the door as he left. "He'll regret that he ever touched me."

Brian looked into the room just as Chris left. "Who are you talking to?"

"No one. Get ready brother because today is the day"

"The day for what?"

"Elimination day."

"Elton, we can't."

"Yes, we can."

Elton pushed his brother into a chair and leaned down to talk to him. "This is the last time he ever touches me or you. When he comes back we will take care of this little problem."

"Elton......"

"Shut up. Not a word. You have no choice here. If you're not with me......." Elton produced one of his knives. This one he called Susie. "Susie will have to come and visit you."

Elton placed the knife point to Brian stomach. "It would be a shame. I really need you."

"Why can't we just leave?"

"And where do we go brother? No. The whole world is screwed up right now and there is no place to go. I'm not going to die from some damn flu. It's better if we stay put for now. Keep everything quiet and no will be the wiser."

What Elton didn't tell Brian was his plan, a plan that didn't include him. Once Brian helped him and he was no longer useful, he would take care of him.

"Elton, listen to what you're saying. We can't do this."

Elton placed Susie next to Brian's throat. "Once and for all, yes we can."

The two brothers sat in the front room waiting for the sun to go down and the night to turn black. Brian was the first one to break the silence.

"Did you put that Michael kid in the basement?"

"Yeah. Gunda is next. I'll leave her for the rats after I'm done with her. I want to get rid of her too."

Brian couldn't believe what he was hearing; he jumped up from his chair and confronted his brother. "She's just a little kid. Why?"

"Because she saw us with Lise. She probably doesn't know it was her mother, but she knew it was a body alright. Right now she's too scared to say anything, but that will change. She'll eventually talk and I have to take care of her before she does that. She's a threat to us."

Brian was beyond horrified. He couldn't do this. Elton scared the hell out of him, but killing his parents and that little kid upstairs scared him even more. He couldn't believe that Elton wanted to kill her just because he thought she saw them.

"I won't do it."

Elton stood so close to Brian then he could smell his bad breath. "You will. Now, I need for you to shut up and sit down."

Brian went back to his chair where he sat for about 20 minutes and then couldn't stand it anymore. Sitting in the dark with his stomach turning and waiting to kill someone was too much for him. He was sweating and jumped at any little noisy heard.

"I have to go to the bathroom."

"So go."

Brian escape to the bathroom, closed the door and sat quietly on the toilet seat. He put his head in his hands and shook violently.

"God! He's crazy."

While Brian was trying to decide what to do, Elton waited silently in the dark. He could be very patient. His patience was rewarded when he heard steps from outside the door. He waited in anticipation.

He called in a whisper towards the bathroom. "Brian."

It was too late for Brian; the front door was slowly opening. The light from the hall pierced the darkened room. Elton quickly slipped behind the front door.

A weaving figure staggered into the room and belched. Elton silently followed behind him. He raised Susie above his head and sunk the knife into the back of his father. When he fell, Elton continued to stab him until there was no movement. He wasn't even breathing heavy after he was done. He laughed and flipped on the light.

He walked over to the body and was surprised to see that it wasn't his father. His mother lay before him in a pool of blood. It was dark in the room and she was in black slacks and a jacket, he had assumed it was his father. Underneath the jacket she had on a white blouse that was quickly turning red. He shrugged.

"You had to die too, but father should have been the first."

Brian stood a few feet away from his brother. He was staring at his mother's body in horror. He hadn't thought that Elton would truly go through with it. His father, yes, but not his mother.

"You killed her?"

"Yeah. She needed to go. Help me get her out of here. She can't be laying here when father comes home."

"How could you do that? You're sick. You killed mother. She never did anything to us."

"Shut the hell up. I told you they both had to die."

Brian never took his eyes off of his mother and said, "I won't help you with this. You killed our mother." Tears fell from his eyes. "How could you do that?"

"I thought it was father, okay? Go get a sheet so we can wrap her up."

When Brian didn't move Elton hit him in the arm. "Now Brian."

Together they rolled their mother into a sheet and put her into the bathtub. "Go get her purse and throw it in the tub with her."

Brian was so shocked that he did exactly what he was told and brought the purse back and laid it close to his mother.

"We can't leave her there like this."

"The blood will drain this way; it's less mess to clean up."

Brian watched as Elton walked out of the bathroom. He assumed he was going back to wait for their father. He was. He stared down at his mother for a few minutes and then went to her bedroom and opened the top drawer of her dresser. Inside was a small silver box. He took it out, opened it and removed her rosary. He went back to the bathtub and opened the sheet. He placed the rosary around her neck.

"Bye mother. I'm sorry."

~~~

Chris Bounce came home two hours later at 3 o'clock in the morning. Elton was awake and waiting for him. Once again, he stood silently behind the front door. Chris had spent the night playing poker with three of his friends. He had a good night and one over $200. He was slightly drunk when he walked in the door. Elton stabbed his father in the back with Charlotte.

Elton had names for all of his knives. Charlotte had an 8 inch serrated blade and was much bigger than Susie. He felt he would need a larger knife or his father, went back to his bedroom and carefully put Susie away. He picked up Charlotte.

He was right about needing a larger knife. Chris turned and grabbed whoever was attacking him. Elton kicked out at Chris, and heard him grunt, but he didn't loosen his grip. He screamed for Brian to come and help him. Brian was sitting in the bathroom with his hands over his ears.

Elton continued to fight with his father. They rolled across the floor and into the wall. Chris struck out catching Elton just below his left eye. He rolled away from Chris and scrambled to his feet before leaping at him from behind. He raised his arm and came
~~~

down piercing Chris in the neck. He pulled the knife out and hit him again driving it in deeper. Chris collapsed to the floor and once he was down Elton continued to stab him. After he stopped moving Elton rolled him over and plunged Charlotte into his heart.

After he was sure his father was dead he got up and took off his bloody shirt throwing it across the room. He lightly touched his eye. "Asshole." He went to find Brian.

He stood in front of the bathroom door for a few minutes before he started to pound on it. "You can come out now. It's done."

Brian slowly opened the door and looked into his brother's eyes, he was grinning. He glanced over into the other room and saw his father's body.

"We have to get father wrapped up and put both of them at the front door. I need a shower so grabbed mother's legs."

Elton decided to wait until the next night and then get rid of the bodies. After dark he went to find Brian. He was lying in his bed and staring up at the ceiling. "It's time."

Brian looked over at his brother. "He's too heavy. I don't think we can carry him."

"We carried Lise, so we can do this."

"She was a lot lighter."

Brian tried again. "I can't."

"Wait here, I'll be right back."

Elton went down the hall and took Gunda's wagon from underneath the stairs. He went back to the apartment and they loaded Chris onto it.

"I put father's car outside of the door. We'll put him in the trunk and then come back and get mother.

Brian looked back at the body of his mother. His stomach rolled it was all he could do to keep from vomiting. Elton picked up Chris's legs.

"Wake up. We have to get this done."

Elton pulled and Brian pushed the wagon to the back door. Elton opened it and casually walked outside while Brian waited with the body of his father. He was back in minutes.

"It's all clear."

After they deposited the body in the trunk, they went back for their mother.

Elton would drive the car while Brian would sit nervously next to him. He started to mutter, "This just isn't right. It's so wrong. We actually killed them. Our own parents."

"I killed them. Relax, once we dump the bodies its over."

"Dump the bodies! They were our mother and father."

"The operative word here, Brian is WAS. Their gone, get over it."

Brian couldn't understand how Elton could be so cold about everything. He loved his mother, but his father, he found that he was almost as terrorizing as Elton. He had to admit that he wouldn't miss living with the tyrant, but he could have lived with him until he was old enough to leave.

When they put mother in the trunk, Brian stopped to straighten her body. He was afraid that if she was bent in an unnatural position she would remain that way.

"Brian, close the trunk and get in."

Brian slid into the passenger side of the car. He looked over at his brother and asked, "Where did you learn to drive?"

"My gang taught me."

"What gang?"

"None your business."

Elton shut the car lights off as they approached the back side of the Cemetery. He sat staring out of the window.

"What are you doing?"

Elton turned to his brother and said that, "we don't want to get discovered. Now do we? They'll throw us in jail forever if anyone finds out."

"Jail???"

"Relax. No one is going to find out. We have to wait about 20 minutes for the workers to break for lunch and that's when we get rid of the bodies."

"You mean mother and father."

"Yeah, whatever."

~~~

Elton told Brian to stay put and he went to make sure that all the workers had left. When he got back to the car his dumb brother was sitting like a statue in the passenger seat. He banged on the window.

"Come on. Hurry it up."

Elton went to the back of the car and opened the trunk. He grabbed the feet of his mother, but Brian stood next to the trunk not moving.

"Move it Brian."

"Where?"
~~~

Elton dropped his mother's feet and went to Brian. He pointed to the south side of the graveyard. "There's a pile of bodies there. We're going to add these two to that pile, but only if you get your ass in gear. We don't have all night." He snarled. "They will be just two more flu victims."

"I thought this was supposed to be a graveyard. What are they doing stacking up bodies and leaving them?"

"You are so dumb Brian. This is the back side of the cemetery. It's about a mile from the main cemetery. There are too many bodies and they have to buried them all at one time. There are no private funerals because of the flu thing."

Elton spoke slowly and evenly like he was talking to a retarded child. In his mind his brother wasn't much better than that anyhow. Brian was disgusted with everything that he was being forced to do; all he wanted to do was leave here.

"Let's hurry and get this done."

Before they could move Elton heard a familiar noise. He grabbed Brian and jerked him down behind the car. He whispered in his ear, "be quiet. Don't even breathe. We've got company."

Elton crawled under the car and over to the other side. He saw tall man in dirty pants and shirt stop next to a tree. He leisurely leaned against it and pulled down his protective mask. From his pocket he took out a pack of cigarettes. He lit one and inhaled deeply blowing smoke out into the night air. A deep red glow burned from the tip of his cigarette. Elton waited patiently, but didn't think he would ever finish the damn cigarette.

"Hey Doyle." A voice called from the darkness. "Get a move on. Break time is done."

"Be right there."

Doyle crushed out his cigarette, but didn't leave right away. He turned his back and leaned against the tree. There was the sound of a zipper and urine splashed onto the semi-frozen ground. After zipping up his pants he walked off toward the grave site.

Elton backed out from under the car. "We can't do this now. There are too many people around so let's get the hell out of here."

27

When Elton and Brian got back to the apartment it was almost dawn. They got out of the car and went to the trunk. "It'll be light in about an hour so we have to get them out of the car trunk."

Brian asked in a flattened tone. "Where are we going to put them?"

"Down in the basement. We're going to bury them down there. Go get the wagon."

It took almost that entire hour before they managed to get the two bodies down to the basement. Brian looked around at the furnace room. "Now what?"

"We'll take them down to the storage area."

Brian looked down the five stairs and into the next room. He simply said, "I can't."

Elton grabbed Brian by the shirt front. He was angry and tired of all of his brother's excuses. "You keep saying that you can't, but here we are. There is no can't here Brian, you need to understand that we are in this together and that is why you will help me with whatever I tell you to do. We can't leave them in the furnace room where anyone who comes down here could find them."

Adjacent to the furnace room was the storage area. There were five stairs down and a slight turn to the right. They placed the bodies in the corner of that room. When they were done Brian quickly ran out and went up to their apartment.

Elton shrugged and went up the steps into the furnace room. He's stopped, turned and went back to the storage area looking down into it. He walked down the five steps and kicked the dirt floor. He stamped his foot down on it and smiled. "Perfect."

~ ~ ~

"I don't care where you find one Brian. Go break in at Tyler's five and dime if you have to. You should be able to find a shovel in there; they have hardware section in the back."

"Why do we have to bury them?"

"Because we don't want them found. We are stuck here for now because the city is shut down................ Remember?"

Again Elton spoke slowly as if Brian was an idiot who couldn't understand him.

"Okay. I'll go find us a shovel."

Brian didn't say anymore. He got up and went to the closet, took out his coat and slipped into it. Elton came up from behind him and trapped on his shoulder. He hadn't heard him and it startled him.

"What?"

"This is Gloria. Take her because you may need her." Elton held out the 6 inch knife named Gloria.

"Thanks. You're right, I might need help."

Brian closed the door quietly and went down the hall to the outside corridor. He opened it and walked onto the snowy sidewalk. He looked up at the sky and then turned to look at the building that had been his home all of his life. He put his hand in his pocket and felt Gloria resting in there. He took the knife out and dropped it in a pile of snow. Brian looked in each direction and decided that he would go south. He walked away and knew that he would never go back again. The Spanish flu didn't scarc him as much as Elton did.

28

Gunda opened the door for Eddie. She gave him a big smile as she took the groceries from him and place them on the table. He put a radio down next to them.

Gunda turn the radio around in her hands. "A radio? Where'd you get it?"

"From my other house. I thought we could use a little music around here."

"Can we plug it in?"

"We can plug it in right now."

The first thing they heard when they turned the radio on was a report about the continuing pandemic. The report was not good news. They were talking about a second wave of the Spanish flu. The government was attempting to stop the spread of this disease by quarantining people they thought were a danger. They made masks mandatory and everyone who appeared in public without one would be fined. The fines could range between $5.00 dollars to $200; there was also the possibility of a 10 day jail sentence.

The announcer, William Robinson continued,

"The government is authorizing signs to be placed all through the city. These signs will read:

Obey the law and wear the gauze.

Wear a mask or go to jail.

Protect you jaws from septic paws.

Gunda looked up at Eddie and asked, "What does a second wave mean?"

"It means that the flu problem is still with us only it's a little bit different."

"Different how?"

Eddie wanted to keep it simple so that she would understand. "When the Spanish flu started it was a certain kind of germ. Now, most of that illness is gone, but from it another germ has developed and that is the second wave."

Gunda thought about it for all of a minute. "Can we try to find some music? I'm so tired of this flu."

"Absolutely."

Eddie and Gunda listen to the radio while he prepared dinner. Michael wandered in and sat down in the kitchen chair staring at the radio. He started to giggle. Mabel soon joined them; Gunda placed her on the chair next to Michael. Just as they were finishing dinner Jaden came in. Eddie immediately got up and made him a plate.

Jaden sat down after kissing each child on the head. He was so tired that eating was a chore. He looked down at his plate and laid the fork down.

"Tired?"

"I don't know how much longer I can do this."

"Children, why don't you take the radio and go rest in the fireplace room."

"Okay Eddie. Come on Michael. Take Mabel's hand and I'll get the radio."

After the children left Jaden pushed the food away. "It's getting worse all the time. Every day more bodies are being delivered and we can't keep up. Two more men in the crew have come down with the disease.

It scares me Eddie; I've lost so much are ready. Three of my children and Lise, who knows what happened to her. She wasn't the best wife, but at one point in our marriage I did love her. Now, she has left nothing but emptiness. Then there are my poor little children who will never grow up."

"You're tired Jaden. You need to rest. Take my bed in the fireplace room; it's much warmer in there."

"I have to be back by 6 AM."

~~~

Elton was furious. Brian had been gone for two days. He went looking for him, but he was nowhere to be found.

"The bastard." he screamed.

He thought about the two dead bodies down in the basement. He no longer considered them his mother and father, just two strangers he had to eliminate because they were a danger to him. Even though they were strangers it didn't mean that he could leave them there for anyone to discover. That discovery might lead back to him.

He looked around the apartment and realized for the first time that he was totally alone. There was no one to tell him what to do and no one who would hit him for no reason. He wouldn't have to help his drunken mother to bed. He realized that most of the people in this building were drinkers.

He sat down took off his socks and ran wildly from room to room in the apartment. He screamed at the top of his lungs and jumped on the bed rolling back and forth. There was no one to stop him.
~~~

Elton lay on the bed smiling. He thought he came up with a solution. There were so many drunks in the building that maybe he could put it to good use.

"A nice fire. Anyone of these drunks that live here could've started it. I can bring the place down to the ground and that will be a lot easier than digging graves.

He would have to plan it carefully and make sure he didn't get hurt in the process. Fire could be tricky. He wondered how he could start a fire so that it would burn fast.

Elton waited until full dark before he slipped out onto the empty streets of Chicago. He decided to walk to the local public library because it was unusual for a car to be seen on the streets. He put his hands on the ledge of the window and pulled himself up to look in. He pulled the hammer from his pocket and hit the window ducking so he wouldn't be cut by any glass.

Once inside he pulled out a flashlight and shined it on the rows of books. There was aisle after aisle of them. He went over to the desk and walked behind it. There was a roll of drawers that held index cards directing you to different sections in the library. He went through the cards until he found information about fire.

He walked carefully with the light shined down to the floor so that he wouldn't fall over anything. Someone had been in here before him and made a mess. Books were all over.

After making several wrong turns he finally found the information section in the back of the library. He found three books that he thought might help him and took them to a table. He opened each one and started to search for the information he needed.

He learned that gasoline is highly flammable and would have to be treated with respect. He would have to gather wood, pour the gasoline on it and let it soak in. It was winter, so whatever wood he found he would have to let it dry out before it would be usable.

"Minor inconvenience"

As he read farther, he found an article that told him how gasoline will spread quickly, but he would have to be careful not to splash it on himself or the surrounding area. The fumes were also deadly if they ignited. The article stressed the safety factor and said that it was imperative that you stand back far enough so you didn't accidentally catch yourself on fire from vapors.

There was also an entire page on the smoke factor which basically said to leave the area quickly and get away. "Bet your ass I'll do that one."

Once he was satisfied that he knew enough Elton left the library the same way he came in. He walked through the cold streets and heard nothing but the silence around him. It would be so easy for him to disappear after the fire.

Elton bent down and picked up a branch that had fallen from a nearby tree. "My first piece."

29

Two weeks later:

Elton could hardly stand being in the basement because it smelled of decay. He added the last of the wood he had dried to the pile he had collected. He would wait until tonight to burn the place down, but first he had to get some gasoline. He went out the back door, walked down the street and over to Leland Avenue. He had stashed his father's car in a deserted parking lot. His wasn't the only car there; they were half a dozen others.

Elton went to one of the other cars and opened the gas tank. He took out a rubber hose and inserted it into the tank. He had several glass bottles with him that he pulled out of a paper sack.

He took a deep breath, let it out and then sucked on the hose to bring up the gas. He got a mouth full and started to choke. He spat the gas out on the ground as he inserted the tube into the first glass jar. "That stuff tastes awful."

When Elton got home he went straight to the basement and left the gasoline close to his woodpile. Next, he went back to his apartment. He had missed being away from the apartment because strangely enough he enjoyed being alone.

"Well, the rent is due next week so I couldn't stay here much longer anyhow."

He took a suitcase from his father's closet and packed it with everything that he thought he would need. He would take it to the car and put it in the trunk, then come back and set the fire.

Suddenly, he realized that he smelled like gasoline. He hadn't thought that he spilled any on his clothes, but remembered the article from the library and something about the fumes. The fumes could ignite and burn him alive.

Elton quickly stripped off his clothes and left them where they lay. His next stop was the bathroom where he got into the tub and scrubbed his entire body. He rinsed and scrubbed again. After he washed his hair he was satisfied that he got all of the gasoline off of himself. He jumped out of the bathtub and dressed in clean clothes. He felt much better.

Elton was going to contact his friend Herbie Schwartz. He was one of the guys he hung around with on the streets. He had learned a lot from Herbie and he would be an asset to his escape. Herbie lived with his old aunt, Annie Schwartz. Herbie wanted to escape this dump of a city too, so Elton was sure that he would go along with him. Maybe he could even get him to start the fire.

Elton hatched a plan on the way over to Annie's apartment. They could take what money old Aunt Annie had stashed away. Of course, that would mean killing her, but he could take care of that for Herbie. No reason to leave her alive and let her talk about what happened.

Elton had the $200.00 that he had taken from his father's wallet. His mother had $10 on her. After he searched the house he found $23 in a cookie jar.

In the few weeks that he had been in the apartment alone, he turned it into a total mess. He walked through the apartment kicking a box out of his way. His suitcase was still next to the door.

When Elton stepped outside he looked up at the sky. It had started to snow again. He pulled his coat tighter and walked down the street toward Herbie's house. He searched the streets as he walked along but couldn't find Herbie in the usual places they hung out, so he decided to go over to his apartment.

Elton entered the apartment house and rang the bell to Herbie's apartment. He sprinted up the stairs to the second floor.

He stopped at room 202 and knocked. A few minutes later he heard the bolt pushed back.

Herbie's aunt stood on the doorstep. She recognized Elton as one of Herbie's friends and opened the door wider.

"Hello, Mrs. Schwartz. I come to see Herbie."

To his surprise she started to cry. She waved him into the room and fell into her chair. It always made him uncomfortable when women cried. "Why are you crying?"

"Herbie, my little Herbie."

"What about him? Where is it?"

"With God. The flu took him two days ago."

Elton backed out of the apartment, leaving quickly, the last thing he wanted to do was stick around and watch some old lady cry.

"Well, Herbie's out."

~ ~ ~

Elton waited until 1 AM before creeping out of his apartment. He had already taken his suitcase to the car, now it was time to act. He wanted to escape from here tonight.

The only thing he regretted was not having time to torment Gunda more. After tonight she would no longer be a threat to him so he put it out of his mind. He looked around to make sure that there was no one around him or walking in the hall.

He ducked under the stairs, moved the wagon and opened the basement door. The smell hit him immediately. He would have to work fast before he threw up.

Elton stacked the wood closer to the furnace leaning part of it up against it. He opened the large door on the furnace, but wasn't careful enough and burned his hand on the hot door.

"Dammit." He screamed and waved his hand up and down.

He soon forgot his injured hand and continued to stack wood against the furnace. He stood back and looked at what he had accomplished. He fished into his pocket for a match and discovered that he had forgotten them.

Elton opened the basement door and looked out to see if anyone was there. It was very dark and he saw no one, but when he came out from under the stairs he ran straight into Jaden. He quickly hid his hand in his pocket.

"Mr. Michelsen." He said turning on the charm. "You're coming home very late."

"We're working in half shifts. It's late, Elton, why aren't you in bed?"

"I was going to use the phone. My father likes me to check in with him and waits at the pay phone by his job."

He wondered if Jaden had actually seen where he came from, but decided he didn't because he turned to the stairs and started to walk up.

"Good night."

"Yes Sir. Good night." Elton said and started for the public phone down the hall. Once Jaden disappeared from view, Elton went back to his apartment for the matches.

He search for the matches and finally found them in the kitchen. They were in a drawer that his mother kept all kinds of strange things.

His hand stung and hurt so he went to the bathroom and ran cold water over it. He felt instant relief once he put his hand under the faucet. He could see the palm of his hand was already blistering from the burn. He looked in the cabinet and found nothing to put on burns. Every time he removed his hand from under the water the pain came back.

"Screw it!"

Minutes later he was back in the basement. Since he had soaked the wood earlier everything was ready. He put some of the wood that had been soaked closer to the door of the furnace. He lit the match and threw it at the wood. Elton waited a few minutes until the wood started to burn before slowly backing out of the basement. He ran down the hall and went out the back door. In five minutes he was at the car on Leland Avenue. He grinned; he had money in his pocket and was now free from everything in his past. A knew start.

Elton would never see his future. He had planned for everything except for one thing. His future was that he would die alone in his father's stolen the car of the Spanish flu. When he went to Herbie Schwartz's apartment he contacted the flu from Aunt Annie who had died that night.

Elton was on the run for two days and lived in the cold car. He had gone approximately one hundred and fifty miles from Chicago when he felt ill and stopped on the side of the road in rural downstate Illinois.

Elton become so sick he was unable to get help for himself and died alone in the car. The 1918 serial killer of Chicago would never be found.

30

When Jaden came home Eddie left to go check on his house. He hadn't been home in over two weeks. He told Jaden that since it was late he would come back in the morning, in time for him to go to work.

"It's late Eddie, don't you want to stay here tonight and check on your house tomorrow?"

"I don't want to leave the children alone. It's better this way."

~~~

Gunda rolled over and coughed. She was aware of a strange smell in the apartment. She rolled over, then jumped up and was instantly awake. She shook her brother.

"Go away."

"Michael, get up. Michael, get up. Hurry. I have to wake father."

When Gunda ran out of the room, Michael lay back down closed his eyes. She ran to Jaden's bedroom and jumped up on the bed shaking him. "Father, wake up."

"What's wrong?"

"I smell fire."

Jaden quickly got up from his bed and pulled on his pants. He immediately was hit by the smell of smoke.

"Get your brother and sister."

Gunda ran back to the fireplace room that they still were sharing. She shook Michael again. "Fire, Michael. Hurry."

Michael leaped up. "Fire? Where?"
~~~

"Stay here."

Jaden went to the door of the apartment and opened it. He could hear screaming from below. Orange flames were licking close to the stairs. In a few minutes the stairs would be involved, there would be no escape this way. He went out onto the small landing and looked down. It was too far for them to jump. He went back into the apartment and closed the door. He ran to the fireplace room where the children were waiting.

"Gunda, you and the children are going down the window stairs."

There were two big windows in the fireplace room. They were located on either side of the actual fireplace. This was their secondary route out in case of emergencies. Outside of the window was an iron staircase that went down into the alley. Most of the large apartment buildings had them because they were required to have two exits and this was considered the second one. It was commonly called the fire escape.

"Gunda, you take Michael and Molly and start down. I'll follow behind you."

When Jaden went to open the window he found that it was stuck. He put all his effort into it and tried again with no luck.

"Wait here."

Jaden hurried back into the kitchen and got a chair. Smoke was already floating under the door of the apartment as he hurried back to the fireplace room. When he got there he lifted the chair over his head and slammed against the window. He was astonished that it didn't break. He tried again and nothing happened. It took him three more tries before he actually broke the window. He lifted Gunda out first, then Michael, and Molly who went last. She grabbed onto Jaden crying.

"Molly, you have to go with Gunda. Hold her hand and be very careful."

He handed her out to Gunda. "Go. Be careful. Take care of Michael and Molly. I love you children."

"Father." Gunda yelled. "Come with us."

"I'll be right behind you. Go now."

Michael didn't like the steep steps and sat down; he started to ease down from one step to the other. Gunda held tightly to Mabel's hand and helped her down the steps. It was a slow process.

"Michael, hurry it up. Get up and walked down."

"I can't. It's too high. I'll fall."

"The building is on fire. You have to go faster."

Gunda heard a roar from the building as it shuddered. She looked up the staircase for Jaden, but didn't see him coming. The staircase suddenly shuddered and then shook. She grabbed Mabel.

"Mabel, are you okay?"

"Scared."

"I am too, just keep moving."

Michael was ahead of them. Smoke was pouring out of the building and Gunda could hardly see him. He yelled back at her.

"The steps run out."

When Gunda got down to the end of the staircase she saw that the staircase didn't reach all the way down to the alley. They were good 3 feet from the ground.

"How do we get down?" Michael asked.

Mable grabbed onto her legs and screamed. Gunda shuttered. "I don't think we can."

In the distance Gunda heard a siren and knew that the fire department was coming. She looked down at the ground and it seemed far away.

"Help! Michael, call for help."

The two children started to yell. Just when Gunda thought that they would have to jump and hope for the best she saw Buford Goode running down the alley.

"Buford." Gunda called to the little boy.

Buford stopped and turned around looking up. "What you doing up there. Come down."

Buford lived in the apartment building next store. He was six years old and often played with Michael.

"Buford, go get some help. It's too far for us to jump. We can't get down from here."

The little boy pointed to the building, "your house on fire."

"Buford go get someone. Tell them we need help and bring them here."

"Okay."

Buford ran down the alley and disappeared around the corner of the building. Michael put his hand against the building and pulled it back quickly. "It's hot."

"Don't touch it. Come over here as far away as you can."

Gunda looked back up the staircase hoping that Jaden would be coming, she saw nothing but smoke. It seems like a long time before Buford came back. He brought with him his 11-year-old brother, Chester.

"Chester we can't get down. It's too far."

Behind them the building roared and crackled with the fire, they could hear several explosions coming from inside. Chester decided instantly that there wasn't time to get anyone else.

"Take Molly by the hands and lower her down. I'll catch her."

"Molly, sit on the bottom of the step and I'm going to lower you down to Chester."

"Noooooooooo!"

"You have to. I won't let you fall. Here, take my hands."

Gunda lay across the bottom step and stretched her arms out as far she could so that Mabel would be closer to Chester. She lowered her down and Chester took her by the legs and slid her to the ground.

"Michael next."

Gunda did the same thing with Michael and lowered him down into Chester's waiting arms. Chester turned to his little brother, "Buford, you, Molly and Michael run down to the street. I'll help Gunda down."

"Come on Gunda. I won't let you drop."

Gunda turned around and eased herself over the step. She dangled for a few seconds until Chester grabbed her. They both fell to the ground together.

"You okay?"

Before Gunda could answer they were overcome by a herd of rats running from the building. Gunda screamed and bolted to her feet. Chester took her hand and pulled her along the alleyway with him. The rats were running close behind them.

She heard the windows behind them breaking from the intense heat, glass rained down on them. They continue to run until they were in front of the building. Gunda looked around for Michael and Mable.

"I don't see them."

Chester looked back at the building and took her hand. He knew they had to get away from the building before it collapsed. He led her across the street.

"We'll try to find them."

They searched throughout the crowd of people on the sidewalk calling for them, but couldn't find either child.

"Chester, over here." Buford screamed. "Over here."

Michael and Mable were with Buford. Michael was holding tightly on to Mabel's hand. Gunda was so relieved to see them that she almost cried. The five children continue to watch as the building burned. Gunda knew in her heart that Jaden probably hadn't made it out, but she wanted to search one more time.

"Chester, did you see my father?"

"No. Was he in the apartment with you?"

"He was supposed to follow us down the iron stairs, but I don't see him anywhere."

"You stay here. I'll walk around and see if I can find him. Buford, you stay here too."

While they waited for Chester to return the fire Department arrived and immediately went into the building. Fire trucks filled the streets and men continue to run into the building. They were making an attempt to save the remaining residents.

A man ran out of the building with his clothes on fire. Three men that had been standing watching the fire jumped on him taking into the ground. Two of the men stripped off their coats and threw them on top of him trying to beat out the flames. The man screamed as they hit his body.

A few minutes later Chester came back, he went directly to Gunda and said, "I couldn't find him. Maybe he went to the other side of the building."

"Chester. Buford. You come away from there, right now."

"It's my Ma. We have to go."

"Thanks for looking for my father Chester. Thanks for getting us down from the iron stairs."

"It's okay. Sorry I couldn't find him."

Chester and Buford went to find their mother. Gunda took the hands of her brother and sister. Together they watched the building burn. Everything was lost to them. Gunda felt how cold her sister's hands were. Light snow began to fall. She looked down at her bare feet. None of them had shoes on. All they had on was their pajamas.

Gunda pulled her sister and her brothers close to her as she watched the fire continue burning. The red flames reached upward into the sky. Flames flew out of the windows as it consumed the entire third floor. Everything in the building would be gone.

Everything they owned would be gone, she knew that they didn't have much, but even what little they did have was burned. She looked at the building again and knew that it was going to be a total loss. Nothing would be saved. It had all happened so fast.

"Where are you Jaden?"

It seemed like the fire had a life of its own eating everything in its path. Within minutes the entire third floor where they lived collapsed downward. Thick black smoke billowed up into the air followed by streaks of red yellow flames. The firemen pushed everyone back. The building was a complete loss.

Gunda grabbed Mabel and Michael pulling them through the crowd. She heard a loud crash and turned to watch the building start to completely collapse. She pushed Michael and Mable behind a fire truck and ducked down. Several firemen ran over and huddled next to them. When the building began to roar one of the firemen placed his body across the three children to protect them from falling debris. Mabel and Michael screamed and cried. Gunda put her hands over her eyes and shook violently.

Bricks fell into the street when the whole building finally came down in a heap. Dust and smoke filled the entire area settling over everything. Some man came over and wrapped a blanket around both of the girls and Michael before placing them in a car.

"Stay here." He ordered.

Gunda took the blanket off of her and wrapped it tighter around Michael and Mable. She pressed her nose against the car window and looked at the rubble that used to be there home. Of their entire family they were the only ones to survive. In Mabel's little hand she was clutching the green bear. She gathered them and they left the car.

"You two stay here on the sidewalk and I'll be right back for you. Don't go anywhere."

"Where are you going?"

"I have to see if I can find father."

Michael looked at the crushed building. "He didn't follow us down the iron stairs?"

"I didn't see him. I don't know when he is, so that's why I'm going to look for him."

Men were running back and forth between the building and the crowd. Police were pushing everyone even further back from the building. Michael took Mabel's hand in his and watched as Gunda disappeared into the crowd.

Gunda was very careful as she walked through the rubble. She didn't want to cut her feet, but there was so much debris from the building that she had a hard time avoiding it.

A policeman, Dan Bones, spotted the child and noticed that she was barefoot. She was walking through the rubble of the building. He went over to her, leaned down and said that he was a policeman. He picked her up and took her over to his car.

"You have to be careful. There is a lot of glass around here and you have no shoes on. I'm officer Bones, were you in the building? Who do you belong to?"

"We lived on the third floor."

"Who's we?"

"Father, Eddie, Michael, Mable, and me."

"Where are they?"

Gunda pointed over to a car that was across the street. "Michael and Mable are waiting for me over by that car. Eddie had to go home, and father............ I don't know where he is. I couldn't find him. He was supposed to follow us down the fire escape ladder, but there was so much smoke that I couldn't find him.

Officer Bones knew that there were dead bodies lined up on the other side of the street. He didn't want this little girl to look at them. Someone else would have to look and see if her father was among the dead.

"Do you know how we can contact Eddie?"

"He was supposed to come home this morning. But he wasn't there when the building caught fire."

"Let's see if we can't find him."

Gunda shivered, she was so cold she didn't think she would ever be warm again. "Hold on a minute."

Officer Bones took off his coat and then stripped off his sweater. He placed the sweater over her head and it draped around her. She immediately felt the warmth and the best part of the sweater, it covered her entire body. He put his coat back on and picked Gunda up again. He carried her so she wouldn't have to walk in her bare feet. They went through the crowd twice looking for either her father or Eddie.

Gunda looked all around her and saw the faces of strangers, and then she saw a familiar one. "There." She pointed across the crowd to the left. "It's Eddie."

She called out to him. "Eddie. Over here."

Eddie heard Gunda call out to him and ran to her. She flung herself into his arms hugging and kissing him. He squeezed her tight. "Thank God I found you."

"I was so scared. I thought that the fire was going to get us. Eddie, we can't find father."

The Police Officer introduced himself and explained to Eddie what happened and how he had found Gunda. They walked back to the car where Michael and Mable were waiting. The children ran to him, he gathered them into his arms hugging them.

Officer Bones and Eddie took all three children back to his car that was parked around the corner. Eddie leaned into the car and hugged them once again.

"I want you wait right here for me. Gunda, watch your brother and sister, I won't be long."

"Make sure you come back."

"I'll be back, sweetheart."

Patrolman Bones asked a fellow officer Tyler Mason to wait with the children. He took Eddie over to where they had the makeshift morgue so that he could look at the bodies.

Eddie walked along the line of bodies. The fifth body he looked at was Jaden's. "That's Jaden. Jaden Michelsen."

"I'm sorry."

"Me too, but I'm grateful the children are still alive. I'm going to take them home with me. I'll have to tell them about their father. I'll make arrangements later."

Officer Bones handed Eddie a card with his information on it. "Please either call or stop by tomorrow."

"I will. Thank you for all your help."

Eddie went back to his car and opened the door. He smiled at the three children and said, "It's time for us to go home."

Gunda looked back at was left of the building, nothing but a pile of brick and rubble lay smoldering. The building was dead. It was as dead as all the victims from the epic flu around them.

Eddie put his hand on her cheek and said softly, "we're all going home together."

"And Jaden? He didn't......."

"I know, Gunda. I'm so sorry."

"We have no one now."

"You're wrong. We all have each other. Gunda we're going to go to my house and it will now be your house. Me, You, Michael, and Mable, we are all family now. I'll never let you go."

The pandemic comes to an end.

It was a long recovery for Chicago and the world. The terrible Spanish flu that spread throughout the world started in January 1918 and came to an end in December 1920.

The original flu that occurred in 1918 came back, but it was a much milder event. The pandemic ended in the 2020. The ending came when the people infected died or developed immunity. It was estimated that one third of the world's population had died.

People werc no longer afraid to leave their homes. Slowly, businesses that had been forced to come to a halt came alive again. In time the world recovered.

NOTE TO THE READERS:

Gunda Johanna Michelsen's lived and survive the 1918 Spanish flu pandemic. She was my Grandmother. The family lived in a house with a garden apartment. Gunda lived downstairs from us and her door was always open. There was an enclosed stairwell that led to her place. I have many fond memories of her even though I was young when she passed away.

I wish to share with you just a few of those memories that I have of my Grandma Gunda. She was the most wonderful person I ever knew. I never remember her angry and she always had a smile on her face. She played with me.

Gunda grew up poor, and found herself a single mother at a young age raising three children of her own.

When I was a child I remember her playing the piano at my aunt's house and singing along. If I or any of my brothers or sister were sick she would always bring us a comic book. On Easter we got a chocolate bunny with a dollar taped to it. At Christmas we were all put into the bedroom and she would get out her bells and shake them and my father would yell Ho! Ho! Ho! That is when we knew that Santa Claus had come.

I was around 10 years old when she let me paint a tree on her big living room wall just because I wanted to. She said it was beautiful. Grandma played games, and loved to watch the 50's sci-fi movies with me on television. We would often go to the show together and eat popcorn. The movie was usually a sci-fi or a western.

She would make paper hats out of the Chicago Tribune and then turn them around laughing and saying it was now a boat. We made taffy together and stretched it in her kitchen. Once, the center fell out, but it didn't bother her at all. I remember her telling me to pick it up from the floor because it was clean and no one would know.

Times were slower and quieter back then, she would sit in her chair in the back yard with us. Sometimes she would sprinkle everyone with the garden hose and laugh like she had heard a good joke.

When I was around 13 we went to Washington DC together and toured the White House. We saw the sights of the city and wound up in a museum where there was a huge stuffed buffalo. You could get on it and take a picture. I tried to convince her to do it, but she said that was for someone much younger than herself. I always regretted that I wouldn't have that picture.

I was so blessed to have her in my life; she was not only a source of fun, but a rich source of knowledge. I only wish I had asked her more about her life, but I didn't. I guess I was just too young.

I lost Gunda in 1972 when she died of cancer. It was one of the saddest days of my life. I will always remember the fun and wonderful times we shared together. She always had time for her grandchildren and that time will always be with to me. She was a Grand Lady.

Other Books By: J.W.Becker

The Forever Series:

Dust, Bones and the Forever

Journey toward the Forever

Running into the Forever

Dead is Forever

Ghost Stories:

Murder of a Ghost

Murder of a Blue Lady

Flow River series:

Returning to Flow River and Murder

Hannah's Secret

Greed, Money, and Murder

Murder at 3 PM

Single Books:

Captives: The Story of Wasser Thomas

Trail of Destiny: The Joseph Lansing Story

Time to Play the Game and Count the Dead

Shadows from the Past

Single Books:

The Truth is always at an Angle

Step into Darkness

Shadow in the Darkness

Children's Books:

Welcome to Halloween

Christmas: A Special Time of Year

Stories from My Childhood

The Missing Angel

The Santa Letter